Life's Too Short

In memory of Michael Rubin, Fourteen Hills Press annually publishes a book of exceptional accomplishment by a student or recent graduate. Each book is selected through an open competition by an independent judge.

Fourteen Hills would like to thank to Sean McClain Brown, whose generous donation made this book possible.

The 2016 Michael Rubin Book Award was judged by Iris Smyles.

Cover art by Margaux Crump.
http://www.margauxcrump.com/

Front:
Blushing Bruising I
Salt crystals grown into silk with makeup pigments, oil bar, and prismacolor; 11.5 x 8.25 inches; 2015

Back:
Blushing Bruising II
Salt crystals grown into silk with makeup pigments, oil bar, and prismacolor; 11.5 x 8.25 inches; 2015

Blushing Bruising I first appeared in *Venison Magazine*, Issue 11: Winter 2016.
http://www.venisonmagazine.com/

Cover designed by Danielle Truppi.
Book layout and design by Danielle Truppi and Bradley Penner.

Set in Minion Pro.

"Dámelo o Te lo Quito (Give it to Me or I Will Take it From You)" was originally published in *Transfer,* "Dog Years" appeared in *The Walrus,* and "To Avoid Danger of Suffocation" was in *The Velro Reader.*

Life's Too Short

Loria Mendoza

Winner of the 2016 Michael Rubin Book Award

In memory of my grandmother.

Dámelo o Te lo Quito
(Give it to Me or I Will Take it From You)

We drink salted Modelos from aluminum cans, cut off the bottoms, and bury them among the small crowns of fire I've ignited in the dirt. You call them Dahlias, these toothy fistfuls of tombstone violet and blood-yellow petals, and slugs are eating them. So we bury the bottoms of our empty cans and pour in a sip of beer for the slugs to drown in. We sit outside and devour apples we steal from the yard next-door, so delicious we even eat the cores, sucking the seeds bare before finally spitting them out into the fountains of bubbling beer slime in our yard.

We seem to get all the slugs, you say.

I know it's because our garden is overrun with flowers. There is nowhere to put the cuttings. I'd like to have a vase, bell-gold colored glass, to keep flowers on the kitchen table next to a bowl of apples and a woven basket of pan dulce.

But there is nowhere to put flowers, or apples, or even sweet bread. I count the broken things that cannot be thrown out because they were your father's before he died. The kitchen table is broken, covered in a brown, fuzzy mold, soft as a peach dimple, that makes your eyes water, even when you aren't crying salt into the slug traps when you think I'm not watching. The table groans as if it were alive, as if it were dying, and spits its rotting spores into the air, covering even our sunny windowpanes with a noxious film, while we go without bread because there is nowhere to put it.

A confession lingers in my throat like an unchewed grape. I would rather have bread.

But if he were to come back?

What shoes would he wear? (Does he have the same flat feet as you?) Where would we stay?

Would he step out of his funeral clothes, kick up the bones of his feet on his rotting wood table, spores leaping into the air, filling the cracks of our walls with decay?

The architecture of mourning: a dead man can bring down walls.

All the memories you hold on to like your dead father's broken table—

Dámelo o te lo quito.

Not because I want to deny you, but because you need a place to sit, hang your golden head, and cry.

And because I want to break bread with you in the morning.

Dog Years

The dog would not stop barking, like cuts in the pink of the ear. One leg was a knot of bone, fur, and tumor. It walked in conch shell plateaus, smaller with each turn, herding the crickets out of our yard. I watched as they disappeared into a whirlpool of dirt, dog shit, mosquitoes, hoping the dog, too, would evanesce. The garden died before mother of so much rot, but the dog went right on living, leaving black holes wherever it went. My brother stopped bringing his wife and step-kids when he'd come over. He'd half beg, half scold father, *for the love of God, end this creature's suffering*. But Father would just roll over in his sleep and say *I'm tired*. Brother would say *there are humane ways to do this*, trying to summon his own cruelty to rouse our old man from sleep. But father only barked from the white egg growing in his throat from the years he spent tangled in powdery wires *I raised you, didn't I?* Sometimes, when he sleeps, he mumbles mother's name before biting at the air.

The dog would not stop barking. The body was nearly all tumor. I told myself *it will die any day now*. The food goes mostly uneaten until the blue flies carry it away; he tips over the water bowl walking in his maddening circles without so much as licking the porch. I told myself *this cannot go on much longer* and *it's better to let a thing take care of itself*. I was glad we didn't live in a better neighborhood. The neighbors who did complain never called the police. I looked out the window and watched my boy necklace the dog with his arms like a star circling a black hole. When the dog fell, tired and senseless from being a thing half-alive, my boy picked it right back up, and I could see it in his eyes, how he thought he was helping. I'd wanted life to be like that for my boy. I wanted to ask him *do you know the definition of kindness?* But then there it would be, the barking, like spilt candle wax hardening whatever it touches.

The dog would not stop barking, like the itch of cat's cradle rope rubbing the pockets of your thumbs raw. Mother told me crickets sing most beautifully during the last days of their short lives. She kept some next to her bed in a small wooden birdcage because father said their songs helped him sleep. Mother and I would hunt for them on the first day of spring, when their voices were raw and easy to find. She told me that come fall they would all die, no matter how well we cared for them, and that it was okay to be sad then, for their bodies had once housed the souls of warriors who'd known greatness, which she said is just another word for knowing what it means to be alive. The dog's song is something I will never mourn. I pray that it will die, that the barking will stop. It's the only thing I ask for anymore.

The dog would not stop barking. I didn't have much longer, maybe a few more weeks, and still the dog would not stop barking. The cancer had folded up my insides like origami petals too intricate to unfold. Still, my oldest son would come over, blind to how skinny I'd become under my clothes. I smelled like death, but he probably just thought it was the dog. *What about the dog? It's your dog, after all. For Christ's sake, what about the goddamn dog?* The dog was nearly as big as the house with tumors and hemorrhoids and the entire yard pulled up in its coat, trailing behind him. He looked like the carcass of a piñata. The parties were all long gone. I couldn't remember how many birthdays we'd had the damn dog for. Sixty, seventy maybe? My wife and I wanted to practice parenting with a dog. So much joy, puppy love. And then the mortgage was paid off and they were both dying. As fall crept closer, she and I watched our shadows grow, envious that unlike them, we could not become something greater than our physical selves, blend together, become part of the night that overtook us in our silence. I wept into her neck, she into mine, my throat not yet bullfrogged. *It's time*, she finally said. But I couldn't remember what time it was. I mean, there was our son, still very much a boy, and she was long gone. For a moment I thought maybe time had stopped, but then there was the barking. I felt the egg in my throat crack.

The dog would not stop barking in the high-pitched frequency of snails melting in stereo. The eyes rotted away until one day they fell out at my feet. They shined as bright as mother's opal rings in the last rays of summer sun before drying up and crumbling to dust. I watched as the red ants and blue flies carried away the small atoms that had once beheld our little world. It no longer barked. But still I heard the barking, like so many dawns screaming on my pillow. I asked father *do you hear that?* But he only whined in his sleep. So I grabbed a dusty paring knife with brown bits of God-knows from under a pile of plastic cutlery, old birthday candles, and discarded hospital bills in what had been my mother's utensil drawer. I threw myself around the dog, crying into the malignant folds of its neck, the flesh wringing out the echoes of our requiem, as ephemeral as dog years. I had to use all of my weight to sink the cheap blade through flesh, tumor, muscle, heart, and finally the fifth element that mother said is the last to go. I pulled away and saw my father's egg hatching a song so beautiful, it had to be the crickets.

Hope Chest

I see things on the road and wonder how they got there. A minty copper fork, a pair of pink, foam *chanclas*, green dollhouse bottles of Jameson lined up like bowling pins, a sprouting potato with a faceless clock tail. I know where they'll end up if I don't act fast, so I raise my voice and ask Paho *is that a crack in the windshield?*

Where? Paho asks, turning his wide-eyed gaze from the road to look for a glass spider web.

Never mind, it's just dirt, I lie. I watch the little things Paho surely would have stopped for and collected in the back of his truck disappear in the fish-eye bubble of the passenger mirror. I relax into my styrofoam hole in the passenger seat.

But other times my eyes are not so quick. Paho makes a little cat sound inside of his cheek. *Tich tich! A perfectly good tire! Tich tich! Two chipped-lipped coffee mugs—fine condition!* A box of stubby lipsticks, a stack of mildew-pocked tabloids, a Christmas tree not quite dead, muddy spools of chicken wire, an American flag with 46 stars, *the boots are bad but tich tich! Just look at those laces!*

A plague of litter devours our home bite by bite until we are living in a hot hiccup of garbage. A mattress weighed down with cat-pee and bedbugs gives me asthma and slug skin. A stereo box with Medusa wires electrocutes the cat. Broken windshield wipers, wicker chair termites, and not-so-stuffed animals play hide and seek with the dozen different sets of china Paho has found, all incomplete, chipped, dusty. Jellyroll escaped from his cage two years ago and we never found him. Maybe he found a way out, like Mapa. Or maybe the bees got him.

Every Bulk Eve I barricade my door with mismatched skis and chipped umbrella stands from last Bulk Day, but come 5:00am the next morning, Paho has pushed his way through and is shaking me by the roots of my dreams, herding my sleepy eyes into his pickup with the baby blue doors that don't quite match. My knees play patty-cake at every pothole because I'm too tired to make them behave, and my bed hair is sticking to my neck like flour to a wet plate, but still I am forced to get up and help Paho haul discarded bedsprings, broken flower pots and birdbaths into the bed of his pickup, the cracked iron bird skulls bleeding rust onto everything, as horrified yuppies watch through their bamboo Venetian blinds. When we get home, we haul everything into Paho's pile of found things in the garage, the bees already buzzing at the sweet, eggy smell. Paho bumbles right along with them, digging into an old blender box and tossing up the foam peanuts like wedding rice. I can't watch; the pile of garbage is my father's only refuge, and I think it must be the smell, and the feeling of closeness one can't help but feel when there is no space for anything else, that distracts him from Mapa being gone. I don't want to leave him, not like this, but the smell is giving me a headache. I sneak away and crawl back into bed, pulling yellow pillows on top of myself until I am nothing, and wonder if I'm up to date on my tetanus shots.

Mapa drew a line between the floors of our duplex. She stays upstairs with a hotplate and a single chair tucked under a desk that she uses for a dinner table and wardrobe. I cook Paho's meals downstairs on a burner constantly under siege by moth-nibbled bibles, glittery Christmas wreath pinecones, and bulbless lava lamps so he won't starve. I bring Mapa grilled Velveeta on Tuesdays to make sure she's eating. She's always smoking and reading *Weekly Wonder News* as if Bat Boy and Hairless Ape Baby were her children, not me. Today the hot plate is covered in a fog of dust, and she puts the daily down and eats the sandwich right away. She exhales heavily through her nostrils as if to say *yum* and quickly forgets I'm there at all. When she is done she licks the buttery crumbs caked to her fingers one by one while gazing at the headline, ANCIENT PHOTO-

GRAPHS OF JESUS FOUND HIDDEN IN RABBI'S GARAGE! I cough, and finally she seems to remember she's not alone.

How's your Paho? she asks with her pinky in her mouth, not looking up.

I dunno, I shrug. *Fine, I guess.*

She rolls her eyes because she knows better before wiping her hands on her jeans. Bored with me, she takes her crystal ashtray, the only wedding gift she's kept for herself, and dumps the butts in the toilet. She sprays Windex into the tray and scrubs it until it squeaks before lighting another Pall Mall.

Mapa?

¿Qué, niña?

I try to steel myself by locking my knees and elbows before asking. *When are you coming home?*

But she only wipes her fingers across her sandwich plate and makes a crumby cross on my brow to remind me that I'm no better than the ash at the tip of her cigarette.

—————

One morning, Paho brings home a cedar chest as long as a casket, green and legless. *For you, mi princesa! Your very own hope chest!*

I stare at it, blinking. *What's a hope chest?* I finally ask. Paho's eyebrows slip down their bones like I'm loca.

Didn't your Mapa ever teach you about hope chests? He asks. But the only thing I've learned from Mapa is how much money to keep saved under the bed for an abortion and how to write a capital L in cursive, *like a woman leaning away, getting ready to run.*

I open the chest and find a baby sock and a bridge piece like the one mi abuelita used to wear before it got caught in her throat and wouldn't come up so the doctor had to push it all the way down with a popsicle stick. I make Paho look inside, hoping this will be the time he realizes that some abandoned things should stay abandoned.

Hey, tich tich! A gold tooth! He picks up the bridge piece and runs outside to examine it in better light, leaving me with the baby sock. I carry it down to the alley, to the garbage bin, and pray Paho doesn't see it, doesn't dig it out and bring it back into the house.

Paho must be feeling brave, because when I come back from the alley he is at the top of the stairs yelling at Mapa, bouncing around her screen door like a hot fly.

A daughter needs to know these things! And it's her mother that's supposed to tell her! I don't even know what you put in a damn hope chest!

You're sick, Patricio. You make me sick. You smell like fucking garbage! And look how the bees follow you!

They don't sting!

And what the hell is that? Is that a tooth?

Yeah, well maybe I could spend more time taking care of myself if you helped out with our daughter!

Why does she need a hope chest? What's she got to put in it? That fucking tooth?

Mira! This is a gold tooth! ¿Entiendes? Just—Be a better mother to your daughter, okay?

An hour later, Paho has scrubbed out the felt bottom of the hope chest with the last drops from five or so old bottles of dog shampoo he's been saving for years, dried it with Mapa's old Avon hairdryer, and tossed in some old cardboard trees that say SMELL GOOD SELL GOOD, muttering to himself proudly how he knew these would come in handy. Paho moves it into my room and tells me to leave it open to finish drying, even though it still smells a little sour like baby. But in a few days my whole room smells as sweet as Home Depot from the red cedar wood, like what I think one of the new homes Paho has built would smell like. The scent is so strong that I'm worried it will bleed out and be gone forever, so I shut the chest and only open it a few seconds each day to take a deep breath that I hold until I can see the dust leave my eyes in a parade of reds, whites, and blues.

Mapa, never one to be upstaged, comes into the house and takes all the photos of Paho out of the albums and frames. She gets his wallet from the cookie jar and throws everything—his license, money, Costco Club Card, my baby pictures, and everything else with his name on it—into a can of paint, seals it, and hides it in the garage under Paho's ninety other cans of paint and calls ICE. Two days later, Paho comes home with an NTA in hand and deep grey half moons under his red eyes. He chokes on a sob as he hugs me and counts all my fingers and toes like he used to. He doesn't go upstairs to yell at Mapa like I thought he would, but buries himself in the dirty laundry on the couch and sleeps through dinner. I stop bringing Mapa food so she will have to come out, will have to listen to me yell for once. But she is used to not eating, not listening. I see her leave in a private rush to get bread, butter, and her magazines from the Quick Pick. I jimmy into her room through the small window in the bathroom. It takes three good tries and all my strength, but I finally break the crystal ashtray on the concrete floor. We have fifty more ashtrays downstairs in one of the dishwashers if she really wants one. I secretly hope that she will come, that she will forgive me when she sees we are broken, too.

A few tongue-biting days later is Bulk Eve. I'm scooting the chest inch by inch towards my barricade when I get the idea. I wait until I am good and sleepy, and then place a grandmother-pink satin throw pillow stained side down in the chest, climb inside, and shut the lid. A few hours later, I wake up when I hear Paho. He whisper-sings my name as he tiptoes in, and I hold my breath and stay extra still, even though my skeleton feels like an out-of-breath accordion. I hear him rustle my bed sheets and stomp out. A while later, when I hear the whine of his pickup rolling away, I figure it's safe to come out. I push the lid up but it's like my finger bones are too soft. I wait for the click of the lid as I push harder, but there is only a boxful of silence. I feel lightheaded, disoriented in the black darkness. I wonder if I'm in the paralysis of a half-dream, when I hear the floorboards creak. I know Paho is long gone, that he won't be back for hours. I call out for Mapa, thinking she's finally come. But there is nothing. I call again, *Mapa, Mapa!*

Mija?

Mapa, I'm locked in the chest! The wooden lid creaks inward, as if something heavy has sat on top of it. I start to scream, but somehow it comes out as a throaty pant, my lungs tingling with faux pine.

Mapa, help! Get me out! Mapa's voice sounds soft and close. She is cooing right into the wood.

Stay niña, stay. Under her voice I hear a soft hum, the buzzing of the bees. Somehow they have found their way into the wood. I feel them crawling up my legs. *Mapa, I can't breathe!* My ears are pounding as Mapa nails my coffin shut. *This is what a hope chest is for*—she shouts breathlessly from her efforts.

Mapa, I can't see! The bees swarm above my head, crawl into my mouth, sting my tongue. Their buzzing sounds like breath, gasping, *Paho, Paho, Paho.*

To be filled with the love of a mother's warmth.

To Avoid Danger of Suffocation

I put my head in a yellow plastic bag from the dollar store and try to breathe. I wonder what I brought home in the bag. It smells like bubblegum, but I never buy bubblegum. Bubblegum pulls out your teeth, smack by toothsome smack. But I can't remember what I bought from the dollar store that would have been in this particular bag, because everything I buy comes from the dollar store: cotton balls that aren't really cotton, detergents that always leave my clothes and skin a little blue, and light bulbs that burn out so fast it hardly seems worth it to buy them at all, so I finally let them burn out, one by one, until I am sitting in darkness, breathing inside a yellow plastic bag that smells like bubblegum. Clusters of static pop tiny flames with every shudder of my mane, lighting up the yellow film and my salamander eyes with an unsustainable light. The burst dilutes each time like the cheap flash of a Kodak. *What are you doing? Just what the hell do you think you're doing?* I hear a voice say. It sounds muffled and directionless in the bag.

There is something about you that is ███████, like you might have a knife in your pocket or maybe have read every book. We alternate sitting behind one another on our regular route to the pier. Pretty soon, I am falling in love with the slope of your neck, how it melts into the fine line of your collarbone, the hairs there like ice coming off coat pockets.

One day, I notice we are walking down the beach like an old couple that has walked together down the same street their entire lives. You point to my bruised legs, and I tell you about my dark apartment, the odd hours I keep. You tell me about a new planet that's just been discovered, TrES-2b, the darkest planet, blacker than coal.

It doesn't reflect any of the light that shines on it, photometrically speaking.

I wonder how anyone could've found something so small and dark inside something so big and dark. I think of the long, desperate nights when I couldn't find the doorknob in my own room, waiting with sleepless thirst for daylight to spit in my eye.

Transit photometry, like when something dark passes in front of light.

You try to explain it to me with eager detail. You've mistaken the opaque fact that I live in darkness for a transparent longing to surround myself with it, when here I am, under the light of the moon with you.

It was like a fruit fly passing in front of a car's headlights.

I can only say *whoa*, feeling as if a horse has galloped away from under me. But what I want to say is *what was like a fruit fly?* But I see you are waiting, imploring me to understand, and already I feel a great loss between us through your impatient, soliciting eyes.

I want you to turn around. I want to lick the brine from the back of your neck, to draw lines between the freckles I doubt you even know are there with my fingernails. I want you to shake your head yes and no so I can calculate the Doppler motion of the sun-bleached hairs trailing down the atlas of your spine. But you gesture towards the sea, and I find myself awkwardly stumbling forward in the wind-combed sand, away from the map I had drawn for myself.

It's dark out, and the sea is drunk on moonlight. It throws up a salty glow onto our feet. I lose a shoe to the waterlogged sand, which tries greedily to drink my whole leg—*roughly fifty-five percent water*, you say. When I pull it out, the other forty-five percent makes an obscene smack in protest. You haven't heard. You're naming the autumn constellations like they were classic cars you once owned. The smack is still ringing in my ears. I tell you how I've dreamed my teeth are loose so often that I can't remember whether or not they really are.

Let me see, you say, pointing at the thin space between my lips, where too often words escape without being heard. I learned early that if I speak quietly enough people will lean in closer. The sudden intimacy thrills me.

I open my mouth, baring every bone to you. You knock on my teeth like a polite dinner guest. When none fall out, I want to kiss you, but you are no longer leaning towards me. The back of your neck falls away from me like the constellations whose names I've already forgotten. Your laughter falls behind you, filling the dark bowls of your footprints in the sand.

I snatch the plastic bag off of my head and feel the pinprick of static clinging to my scalp like sand. *Come in*, I say to the darkness I believe to be at my front door. I hear the click of brass against brass. Your voice mumbles *it's locked*. I reach out my hands, moving, I hope, towards the eclipse of the exit. And, all too suddenly, I get it: a fruit fly passing in front of a high beam lamp.

Finger Bone Scissors Beat Nylon Rock

I decided to sleep with you the moment you tried to sell me a dead parrot, before you called your mom in the bathroom to ask her:

"Who the fuck is Mick Jagger?"

Remember that night? I almost hung myself with the porcelain rope of the toilet bowl. You thought I'd died.

When I came to, the room was spinning, not from the alcohol, but from you rolling me up in quarter turns in your alpaca rug.

I started to laugh from the pit of my uterus, or, should I say, hysterically. This is how I'd once said I wanted to die: disposed of, searched for.

You unraveled me and we couldn't stop fucking. We threw our clothes out the window under a bloody moon, and our bodies became celestial mimes, forming straight glowing lines, slipping into each other's shadows, moving the night deeper into dark.

We awoke in a donjon of ice. I looked out the window trying to find that cold that had so easily found us. There was a mule in the middle of the road, and the rising sun in its eyes was softer than our broken-bottle hangovers, and I knew we'd run out of things to talk about when you could only say:

"Well. Let me know about the parrot."

Arachnology

You're peeling chilies in the kitchen. I'm peeling my panties off the floor. I wad them in my fist and shut the bathroom door behind me. I hang my head between my legs and try to exhale my little doubts about us. There's a spider at my feet, the size and color of an old piece of gum that's been stuck to the sidewalk for years. I watch the spider tumble across the tile, picking up dust and pubic hairs. It's dead. All those skin cells and hairs from all the women you've fucked, luminous here between my bare legs. Some tumbleweed. I'm not the type to scream at insects; not dead ones anyway. I wish I were. I wonder: would you come running into my web? Or would you see through my intentions, thick as the walls between us?

Uh-oh

In those days it was hotter than we'd let ourselves be familiar with or comfortable in, as if we could cross our arms and keep the season from entering us in that loose-knotted manner. I would sit at my desk, a foot from the bed in which we slept, in our tiny shadow of a room, and write. Sometimes I just sat, arms crossed, and listened to you sleep. You seemed colossal in your sleep, the stillness of your body filling our dark room with a silence heavy and brittle as a broken wing.

Then came the bird.

I could never see or name it. It had simply alit from the sky, as birds are wont to do. It made its home somewhere in the mossy divots of our roof, or perhaps in our shallow-rooted pear tree that never gave fruit, or in the soft, rotting wood of the porch steps. I never saw it, never bothered to look for it. Like a fever, the heat dripping down from the bleeding yolk of sun kept me inside. The bird squawked madly and without grace from sunrise until noon, cutting my thoughts apart, so lines of poetry became sharp, black and blue, monosyllabic shrieks on heatstroke-white paper. It was the only bird I'd ever heard there. No other came to answer its calls. Still, it talked and talked.

To whom were you talking, little bird?

The bony, brass bell of that bird must've finally cracked, perhaps eaten by something bigger and meaner than itself, or maybe it just flew away into the ash-gray platform of morning. One day, there were only the two of us sitting in our boxful of silence. I sat at my desk, while you lay, not more than two feet away from me, staring at the ceiling, saying nothing, unmoving. I felt as though I were dead.

When it was time for you to get yourself dressed and go to work at a job you cared nothing for nor against, you'd kiss me goodbye, quick as a knife cut, on the lips, and leave my head hovering in mid-air, as the back of yours vanished like some damned Newton's cradle. At night, you returned, and we would chew thick mouthfuls of silence and unseasoned food made without salt or fat or love before we would fall asleep, our bodies close but not touching.

You slept so soundly each night. On occasion, I would ask what you'd dreamt about.

Nothing, you'd say each time.

No really, I would say, my fingers tapping lightly against the hard bones of your sinuses, trying to tap out the ash of your thoughts, which you kept to yourself, always to yourself.

No, really. I don't dream. Never have yet, anyway.

There was a time I pitied you for the quiet stillness that nested upon the heavy white egg of your dreamless, unhatched sleep. I sought asylum in dreams about my family, sitting across from them at a picnic table, barefoot, a girl again, eating the warm biscuits and slow-cooked roast my mother served every Sunday, rolling piping hot corn, slick with sage butter, in my hands, the herbaceous oil dripping down wrist to elbow. Once, a dog appeared, looked at the meat in our hands, my father yelling, stop, my mother yelling, hurry up, noises of plates piling on the table like worry. Uh-oh, I'd said, still as a knickknack as the dog approached my legs, before waking, my fear turning ravenous, the cold teeth marks on my thigh no longer sparking at the nerves. But since the bird left us, I find myself dreaming only of skies made of dark, feathered wings and a cold, golden, bird-eye moon that turns on a rusted axis, its mad squawking filling the morning, always the same morning, when you shake me awake by the roots of my dreams and tell me I've been talking in my sleep.

Who were you talking to? you ask.

But I can never answer, can only slip my limbs, covered in the slick oil of bad dreams, out of your grasp, and ask you did you do it? Did you finally dream?

Where did you come from, little bird? What about this place drove you away? Is there a clock in all of us that tells us when it's okay to fall from the sky? I listen for the ticking of that clock, but there is only the voice of a little girl who says, uh-oh.

Uh-oh.

Ink and Flesh

There's a crow in my bed making a nest of my hair. He pecks at the freckles dotting my neck. My teeth grind down on saliva, bone. I forget to swallow, but the words go down, while bruise-colored sheets rise up between my toes.

"We've run out of things to say to each other," you said. And just like that it was true.

The crow's feet remind me of your nova-blue eyes and your single feather of ink and flesh, a whirlpool of barbed wire tattooed into your skin that I wanted to wrap around my body.

The crow listens to my stories, pins my poems on the walls, asks me for cigarettes. I must have left the window open tonight. The match won't catch. I hold it against my palm to protect it from the breath of night. It burns a hole in my bundled skin, makes lace of my palmistry. I wonder, have you found some other hand to hold?

I finally smell the sulfur and drop the cold match. My mind wanders back from you in time to see the crow tugging at a cord of flesh hanging down my thumb. He flies great circles around the room, undressing me within seconds. I see my skin lying in a heap on the floor like an old pair of ripped fishnets. He settles in what he has gathered of me, tells me, no, he never loved me. He's only a crow. He only wanted to roost in my skin, to snap me up like worms. I pull him out of the drying brambles, wrap him in my glowing limbs, but the wound is too fresh. I remember a name, a face, before they fly out the window.

Eulogy for Nicolas Zschiesche

Nicolas Zschiesche died early this morning from heart failure. Or maybe it was liver or kidney. There will be no autopsy because he's been declared "definitely dead, with good riddance."

Surviving him is his wife Ulloa, who couldn't be happier to finally have the bed all to herself. Mr. Zschiesche rarely groomed and could no longer touch his toes. Consequently, his toenails were always too long and cut his wife's calves to ribbons in his sleep. He was a thrasher, a teeth grinder, and a mouth breather, and for these reasons, Mrs. Zschiesche emphasizes that she really couldn't be happier to finally be rid of the sad sack.

Preceding him in death are his mother and father, sister and brother, and two twin sons from a previous marriage who hated him desperately, especially so in those final moments just before their bodies and souls flew from the windshield when their father's drunken hands slipped from the wheel to take off his belt. Nicolas Zschiesche died early this morning and there is no one to blame, his only regret.

Carpet

"Zuzu! Come clean this fucking shit up!"

My sister, Ninny, is not pleased with the paper diamonds littering the shag carpet in her room. I didn't mean to upset my sister, still on edge from the time of year, but the cutout scraps from my coffee filter snowflakes seemed to have taken root in the gnarled carpet. What does she want me to say? They got away from me. Like the time. And the vacuum has disappeared. Everything of Mom's has disappeared over the last year: ironing starch, hairbrushes, her canaries Juju and Olive, jewelry that never saw outside of her vanity until after she died, four silver spoons, one for each child, who are also disappearing. None of us are ever where we're supposed to be anymore. It's Christmas day, and I don't even know where any of my brothers or sisters are, except Ninny, and that's only because she's screaming at me. At this time of day the light hits the walls so that even the stains in the wallpaper disappear. Like my mother was never even here.

Somehow a whole year went by without anyone bothering to put the tree away. It sits in our living room, untrimmed. We never got to it last year. That had always been Mom's job. Not the actual decking of the halls so much as making sure Ninny and I did, shushing us from her beige Lazy Boy when we'd bicker, as if on cue, about whether the tinsel or garland went on first, which lights to use: the little whites or the matte-glass globes, whether we should use the star or angel tree topper. There were always too many decisions to make, too many things to fight about. Mom was a Christmas hoarder. Our garage was a plastic, evergreen forest, a new Christmas tree sprouting every year to house her ever-expanding collection of tacky dollar store cheer and Christ paraphernalia. When my brother David finally moved out, she turned his room into a storage room for her dozen Walmart-sized bins of ornaments and garland, including special donut- shaped Tupperware made exclusively to store Christmas wreaths, a half dozen tone-deaf singing Santas, battery-operated shivering snowmen door stoppers, and three rings of jingle bells for every doorknob in the house. She'd been collecting the stuff since we were kids, and when her mother died she no longer held back. It was as if she was trying to replace everything she'd missed out on as a kid by refitting it all into one holiday, like no matter what happened, one day a year she could watch *It's a Wonderful Life* and actually believe it was. Macy's had nothing on our window display. The tiny town my siblings and I made each year had dollar store glitter snow, evergreen branches glued to popsicle sticks, porcelain dolls snug in their porcelain coats, and a tiny grandmother Ninny made out of Q-tips and doll clothes. When she found out she was sick, Mom placed tiny strips of masking tape on the bottom of every single Christmas item, equally dividing the names on the bottom between me and my three siblings.

"You kids are lucky," she'd say, carefully peeling layer after layer of expertly folded white tissue paper from the glittering crystal orbs and baby Jesuses before handing them off to us, one by one. "You won't know what it's like to lose someone and have nothing to remember them by. When I die you kids will always have Christmas. Do me a favor and don't fight about who gets what. So long as everyone gets a little piece of me to remember me by—"

"Don't talk like that," Ninny would always shout. "For Christ's sake, Mom, it's Christmas!"

But Mom barely paid any attention to our protests. She was already leaving us for another world. She'd sit upright as a paper doll on display, high-heels sinking into that ugly, grey-pink shag carpet that she hated so much for constantly offsetting her beige name-a-noun, never able to work enough overtime to replace the rug with something more "Biscuit," "Cream," or "Champagne" and still keep us all fed, clothed, and in school.

"This one's chipped," she'd say of a transparent, red-laced globe.

"Put it in back. Here, Zuzu, 1987. And a 1992 for Ninny. This one's my favorite! Oh wait, no, maybe this one. . ."

Even when most of us had grown up and busied ourselves during the holidays with last minute shopping, unfinished term papers, or wrapping up presents for our own families, every year was the same routine with Mom and her tree. Every Christmas Eve, my siblings, well into their 30s and 40s, would come over and teach their own kids how to decorate the tree, Ninny and I suddenly feeling the need to jump in. "No David Junior, that one's mine, see? 1992. Give me that, honey. Here, you can have Snoopy."

Then one year, Mom couldn't remember where she'd put the ornaments. All the boxes in David's old room were empty except for some tissue paper and loose glitter. When we finally found some of them stuffed into Maggie's old doghouse, she couldn't remember what birth ornament went with what kid. And then she couldn't remember our names. Or hers.

"Goddammit, *now*, Zuzu!"

I head to Ninny's room, the one we shared before everyone else moved out, tired of dad drinking all their drinks and smoking all their smokes after Mom died.

"Want to help me put up the garland?" I ask Ninny, smiling feebly and gesturing towards the sad wads of paper I've strung together with mint waxed floss.

"Fuck your shitty garland. Fuck Christmas. Fuck you." Ninny storms out, slamming the door behind her. It's like when we were kids, but it's not like Christmas. I look down at the scraps, almost braided into the ever-hungry carpet.

I squat down, trying to tweeze out the scraps of paper with my fingernails, but the carpet is tenacious. Mom was right to hate it. I instantly snag a nail in the thick, braided fibers. I comb my fingers through the shag, almost admiring its resilience. Up close, I see that inside of it there are hairs—long, short, pubic, eyelash, animal—yellowed nail clippings, staples, and scraps of food scrubbed into coffee stains. Rather than pick out the tissue paper cuttings, I decide to just rub them against the hairy pulp, using the carpets tenacity to my advantage. The scraps begin to make a sort of snowball against my palm. I ball up the little bit of paper I manage to pull out, bits of hair rolling up with it. I'm about to toss it into the garbage when I see it. A long, silver hair. It glimmers in the light. Somehow the shag carpet has preserved the vibrant silver hue of my mother's hair. The ornaments are still nowhere to be found, nor her ironing starch, hairbrushes, canaries, jewelry, silver spoons, children, but suddenly here she is, a perfect piece of my mother. I hold it under my nose and twist it into a thin moustache, trying to get the last bit of her scent, her texture, something. In a house where everything's disappearing and taking her away with it, here she is.

I go downstairs and forget about the lights and the garland and hang the beautiful, single strand of hair from our old plastic evergreen that no one has bothered to take down. The most beautiful tinsel.

Catfish

I'm sitting alone in the bar, motion sickness pulling my blackened eyes into my concrete-skinned hands. The wall is smeared with what looks like boogers. There's even a little blood in one. The place is a dump. We don't belong to each other, but we are trying to make it work, which is more than I can say about most relationships.

The well whiskey has left me shaking my bruised head. But I remember some things.

I was on my back in the middle of Sycamore Street thinking I should be seeing stars, but there were just lines as my eyes blurred and uncrossed. I learned how hard a man can hit a woman when he wants to hit her hard. Who was lusting after her, you or me? Who threw the first punch? By noon I'd heard it both ways. A man they call The Kid had stepped in. Get, he said, swinging the door open for you. You weren't looking at The Kid, but at me, sucking the blood off of your skinned knuckles, not knowing what to say. Then, The Kid called to me. C'mon Miss, you wanna get outta here? But I didn't. I knew I'd never leave you for some cowboy. Never had yet, anyway. Stupid, The Kid said before walking out. Just stupid.

But who's to say what love is? For all I know, it's the cyst in my cheekbone throbbing under my fingertips, knowing that was the feeling of two people trying to merge their bodies together. Or maybe it's the way you wouldn't touch me after you'd hit me, like dropped crystal that doesn't break, and you're afraid to pick it up and find a crack in the glass, so you just let it collect cobwebs on the kitchen floor. Or maybe love is the skin-cutting grit that gets hiccupped through the cracks of a bone or a glass the second before it breaks. And now my body works hard to digest my own teeth, and I could just wretch my rotten gut into my glass or crown a screaming child.

An old woman sits in the corner of the bar with a pushcart of wilting cabbage, the kind you can buy at Mission and Sixteenth for twenty-nine cents a pound when you can't afford anything else. She cups her thistled chin, the whiskers blinking like dewdropped cobwebs in the splits of tree bark. I realize both of us have probably looked better. I watch as she rubs at the hairs with mushroom-flesh hands blooming with wine-colored stains, the bruises of longevity.

Bones

Scars constellate my left arm like the dusty remains of stomped-out moths. I look at my right arm and laugh at its nakedness. My eyes fall to the deep, telling asterisms in my right hand, the dissected lines like a page torn from your Reader's Digest palmistry book. I don't want to look anymore, but when I try to squeeze my hand shut it's suddenly seized by premature arthritis from overuse of Adderall, cocaine, anxiety meds the colors of Easter eggs, cigarettes, weed, and rotgut tequila. Held halfway open like this, I can see the scars line up where I once held a shard of glass from a broken mirror now pieced back together with painter's tape in my antique vanity. And even though I taped up the wounds and the mirror, it's still seven more years of bad luck. Enough is enough. Enough failed relationships, enough nights of monitoring my vitals, enough eviction and rehab threats. Enough of this trap, this addiction to sadness.

On a bender I watched the entire Dollars Trilogy. Maybe it was the pot, or the whiskey, or the sorrowful, tremolo, mezzo-soprano voice scored by Morricone that got me on my back in the middle of the room, thinking about my life, how death would be sooner rather than later if I kept it up, and all the things I had never done, the hundred dollars I forfeited rather than get on the small plane that was supposed to take me skydiving, convinced I'd have a heart attack in the sky, but somehow, like the Man with No Name, I came to get it in my head that the treasure I've been looking for lies in a grave. Your grave. Maybe it's a quarter-life crisis. Maybe I need to explore the liminal state of death, which, according to Brenda in the Psychological Services building at school, "compels me to self-destructive behavior with its ultimately desirable state of nirvana." Or maybe I just miss you. I haven't felt loved, really loved, unconditionally, since you died. How much of it was missing you, how much of it was me?

I travel the hundred and ninety miles or so west down Highway 29 thinking I will find your grave at last and cover the earth that houses your bones with wildflowers because, after the stock-up of uppers and downers and in-betweeners, I have no money to buy roses, and I think they are tacky anyway, too cliché, and while the plastic shit is cheap enough the flowers will fade unnaturally like an embalmed body. I want to give you something organic, something that will seed and take root while resisting disease.

Half a pack of smokes into the long slog down the one-lane desert road, that is uncannily familiar and different all these years later, sitting in the driver's seat for the first time, the station I've been listening to goes to static, and I turn the dial until *Die Walkure* comes through faintly on a classical station. Back on your salt and pepper living room carpet when I was six, the static of your television speakers blasted Elmer Fudd's rendition, "Kill the Rabbit." I was laughing so hard, but when I glanced back you were asleep in your golden armchair, a dozen near-empty pill bottles on the coffee table at your fingertips, a cigarette burning slowly towards your perfectly manicured, nicotine-stained fingers, as your other hand dangled over the spot where my head had been resting ten minutes before. I slid the Marlboro from between your fingers and stamped it out in an empty sardine can swimming with butts before switching the volume down and kissing you goodnight. I wasn't tempted to smoke it. You'd let me have my first cigarette when I was four. I didn't especially care for it, but even back then I wanted to be like you and all I ever had to do was ask and you couldn't say no. You popped pills and gave me Tums and Smarties so I could imitate you when I asked if I could have some too. If you ate mustard and sardine sandwiches, I had to have them too, though you cut the crusts off mine. Mom was at home taking care of the new baby, and I was glad to be the center of attention. You played favorites, unabashedly. Looking at the pictures, I think it was because of how much more I looked like Mom than my sisters, and how, unlike her, I wasn't harboring the resentment of a neglected child. I didn't hate you, couldn't hate you, because instead of leaving me with a child molester while you went out into the world on adventures, you settled into your old age and let me draw suns and happy girls on your walls with crayons while talking about how handsome Pat Sajak looked that day on Wheel of Fortune.

Mom hated you for it. You were "like a mother" to me, and a wonderful one, but because you had been her actual mother, and had been objectively terrible, leaving her with careless relatives for the first fourteen years, then showing up once a year with enough rent money to live alone in various Austin ghettos with bad locks on the doors and no forwarding address, she was only capable of forgiving you enough to let you in her children's lives when it was convenient for her.

The song begins to crescendo into the final coda, and I pull over, disengage the keys from the ignition, dip them into the baggy hidden under an old coffee cup, and snort a bump. I hear my ex's voice in my head. *Addict. Coke whore.* I try to put the words behind me as I drive away but they trail down the back of my throat with the powder, and I begin to digest them along with the nails I've been biting off. A million thoughts are racing through my amphetamined mind, as the yellow divider lines begin to bleed into each other, the speedometer creeping past eighty-five, ninety, ninety-five, one hundred. The day I heard you'd died, I'd woken up with my eye makeup smeared on some stranger's thigh. I didn't even know his name, or what had happened to the drugs in the empty bags tucked into the corners of my wallet, purse, sometimes even used as bookmarks. All I knew was that the rest of that semester's financial aid was gone, Dad was still out of work, and mom was in debt. The mouths of the baggies seemed to laugh at me with their ziplock teeth when I pulled up my bank account statement, a long telling list of recurrent ATM withdrawals of sixty (an eighth of weed), one hundred fifty (a couple grams of coke), eighty (a handful of narcos), and twenty dollars (three to five Adderall pills, depending on if I got them from Skinny Tony or Martina). There was nothing left. Desperate, I went through the guy's wallet when he was asleep, but there were only three faded dollar bills and a condom. I couldn't fly cross-country back to Texas for your funeral, but the rumors slingshotted back to me from my brother, who'd never left Texas, of the funeral tell-all of your addictions, your adulteries, of your and my mother's rapists. As I hung up the phone, it all made so much sense to me, sitting at my desk staring at the Punnett squares in my biology book, that I was just a repeat, a cliché. I did drugs because they were fun. It brought me closer to you, made me miss you less, by making me every bit as damaged and numb as you must have been.

I light another cigarette with the one I've nearly finished and remember my first college lecture and the professor telling us to avoid all clichés in our writing, the most cliché advice you can give to a writer, and how cliché it was too, I think, that I would fall for my married professor, how cliché that we would have an affair, how cliché that he called the whole thing off, his cliché guilt propelling him to go home that night and fuck his wife good, even taking out the trash afterwards just to show what a good guy he was, only to tell me about it the next day, and how cliché that he thought I'd ever wanted him to leave her in the first place, to inflict that kind of abuse on anyone, how cliché that he himself had entertained the idea, his guilt making him abusive towards me, and I wonder now if he's ever thrown a book at the back of his wife's head. Poor woman. Poor women everywhere. I laugh, looking at the engagement rings I inherited from you crowding every knotted knuckle on my hands. There are a few flakes of blow under the pointer knuckle, and I slide the whole digit into my mouth and suck it clean. My eyes come down from the road, carefully inspecting under each of the fourteen golden rings for anything sizable enough to snort.

You were married that many times in that many states and only divorced three. You were looking for something you never found. Forgiveness, maybe, for leaving your daughter in the shit storm that was your mother's house. Or it could have even been love, always looking for someone to finally choose you over someone else ever since you told your mother about the abuse your brother inflicted on you and she chose him, believing his word over yours. But that might be a bit ambitious. Could you just have been looking for freedom? You spent so much of your life being trapped. And before they knew it, you were a biker queen, a Vegas groupie, a fire dancer, a strip club owner, a sojourner in every relationship and every place you went. I like to think that's why you finally took the last name Guest. It just seemed fitting.

I stop on the highway at a stretch of bluebonnets and remember the picture Mom tore up of you and me sitting in a field just like this on an Easter Sunday long ago. You'd shown up on Friday, as you'd been known to do, without calling, without anyone hearing from you for months, and at times, years. You told the poor, pimply, nervous babysitter who you were and that Mom had given you the a-okay to take me out for Easter weekend. Of course, this was a bald-faced lie, the best kind for your skill set (some say I've inherited your poker face and inability to tell a kind white lie, sparing no feelings for frumpy new outfits or bangs on people that have no business wearing bangs).

In the passenger's seat of your pickup, there was a basket full of Easter eggs, and on the floor sat an Easter tree, a small wicker frame with sugared gumdrops hanging from every branch. We drove for hours down the highway, you tossing your chain-smoked cigarette butts out the window, while I mimicked your behavior, chucking the shucked pastel shells of hard-boiled eggs into the road. We pulled over halfway to San Saba and went fishing in a small ditch. We didn't catch anything but an old shoe sole and some algae, but I'd never been fishing before and I was happy to have caught anything. With Dad in California taking care of his first family and Mom working two jobs, I barely ever made it outside of daycare centers and living rooms, and to this day I still have the pallor of a leghorn egg. Two Motel 6's and three dozen hardboiled and dyed eggs later, we picked up a thin-lipped mustachioed hitchhiker who let us each drink from a thermos of Bailey's, and when we found a stretch of Bluebonnets, it was he who'd taken the picture. You picked one of the state flowers despite the law, and showed me the variation of violets in the petals, pinching the wing petal cups back to show me the sharp, fang-like keel. You told me that when something was so beautiful, it was important to stay on guard. Plenty of people would try and destroy something, you said, just because the beauty was too much for them to comprehend.

When we finally got to San Saba, you took me and the john you picked up to your new place of business: a titty bar pancake house where Mom was already waiting, wide-eyed, sleepless, white hairs in her thick, black mane where there had been none before, furious at you for kidnapping me. It was another year before she softened up enough to allow you visitations, supervised by her. The picture of us in the bluebonnets is gone, and the memories, too, but I remember picking the paper petals out of the garbage like delicate flowers after you died, before Mom caught me and threw them in the sink and set them on fire, piece by piece. My mother, a hard woman, never cried. "Rusts my pipes," she would say whenever anyone accused her of being heartless, dry-eyed at weddings and funerals alike, unlike me, a perpetual and ugly crier, or as you liked to say, "a sensitive child." But since you died, Mom has been a wreck. She can't forgive you, nor can she forgive herself for not forgiving you. She's developed a propensity for hoarding, gained fifty pounds, and, according to my father, who has stopped coming home on weekends and smells like Chanel No. 5 on Mondays instead of my mother's drug store freesia spray, hasn't had sex with him since the day you died.

Mom didn't go to the funeral, either. Not because she couldn't afford it, but because you died of an overdose. "She died the way she lived. A loser." No one said anything to Mom at first. We all knew better than to counter my mother in her state of anger. She locked herself in her bathroom for four days. She took no food, drank from the tub until the funeral and wake were over and done with. Half the time my mother will not speak her name. But the other times, somehow everything you did was funny, enigmatic. The hurt was still there, but now there is something else. Forgiveness. "She died of an overdose. Bless her heart." Or, "If only I'd been there. I would have known to call 911. She might have lived." Sometimes I close my eyes and pretend she is talking about me. Sometimes I think if I could just die, my mother might realize she could get this love thing right between us.

There are no towns or cops for a hundred miles, so I pull over and snort another forty milligrams. I break the pill up with a key and smooth it into lines with my driver's license, bent around the edges from cutting up pills. The gritty line of sky disappears into the rolled-up dollar bill and the sweet paste trickles down my throat. I watch my eyes dilate in the rearview mirror, and the veins under my sunken eyes get bluer.

I jump out and pick as many wildflowers as will fit in the passenger seat of my '88 camper pickup, a gift from Mom and Dad for going longer than anyone in our family without getting knocked up. It looks a little like a sea foam hearse, and the flowers and sickly thin girl in the driver seat don't help dissolve the illusion.

Mom and Dad don't know where I'm going. Dad would never let me drive on any Texas highway without a guy or a gun in the passenger seat, and Mom never let me visit you during your last years alive, convinced somehow that you're the reason she's known how to blow a guy since she was four years old, so I'm sure as hell not telling them I'm finally on my way to make peace with you for the sake of us all. Dad would beat me, surely, which I can take, but Mom wouldn't talk to me for God knows how long. She once went a year because she found a joint in my sock drawer. She didn't inherit your unconditional love for me. While you loved me when I was chubby, skinny, covered head to toe in your fifty-dollar eye shadow running down the street naked because I liked the way my whole body sparkled in the sun covered in the glittering powder, Mom was busy locking me out of her bedroom whenever I got to be just too much, telling me she hated me when I'd have temper tantrums and try to break through her door at night because I was scared of the man outside trying to get inside the house and needed my mommy, and later, she was kicking me out of the house for not being where I said I would be some nights, for being a stupid slut, and I better not get pregnant because I'd probably just dump the kid with her like you had done with her and your mother.

I look at my left arm, the self-inflicted scars exactly like Mom's. That's when I figured out she didn't get them from a car crash, that scars in our family are as genetic as addictions and birth defects, the night my professor accused me of being a coke whore, of fucking every guy in class (when in reality there were only the two), and loving drugs more than him. I was drunk, coked up, and had just chased a bottle of Codeine with a bottle of triple sec. When, in the moment of passion, he had slammed my vanity closed on my stash, broken the mirror to jagged bits, I'd picked up a shard that had fallen out at my feet. "Look," I told him, holding the glass to my arm. "This is how much I love you." I dragged the glass across my wrist and didn't even flinch. I wasn't afraid to prove how fucked up I was. I wanted to be a disaster, wanted to be forgiven for being a disaster. There was something about those scars on Mom's arm that always drew me in, and, in a fucked-up moment, I wanted to feel her pain. Wanted to understand why she couldn't love me no matter what. What did she know about life and love that I didn't? What was it that was keeping us all apart? I wanted to be closer to her, and closer to you. Closer to the heart of the pain that makes you and me you and me.

There is something about the acrid smell of formaldehyde and burger grease that smells like home. When I see nothing but dusty Dairy Queens and faded taxidermy signs I know I'm close. I haven't been here in years—since Mom cut you out of her life, and consequently, mine—and I don't remember the exact address, but in a one-road town there are only so many places you can go, and I find the cemetery right away.

I dreamed you were buried under a live oak just like the one I'm staring at now. I grab all the bluebonnets that will fit in my hands, the spiked stamens cutting into the scars in my hands, and walk to the first cross I see, expecting it to read Franny Guest. Instead, I'm greeted by Samuel Bortz, Beloved Husband and Father. I don't know him, but we're probably incestuously related somehow. Menard has always been that kind of place. The only advancement they've made is discovering meth. Inbred, dough-faced meth heads walk around this ghost town like zombies, but with worse teeth.

Starting inside the Bortz family, I move in a conch shell pattern around the entire cemetery, walking on the graves, bluebonnets spilling out of my pockets on each one for penance. An hour later, the sun has moved too close to the earth. My skin begins to burn from all the toxic sweat, the drugs finally leaving my system. This is the longest I've gone without a snort, swallow, puff, or sip, and everything begins to look clear and dreamy as a vivid memory. Has the sky always been so blue that it hurts even to look at it? My teeth grind down. My pinkies go numb. I pat down my pockets and find my lighter, look in my pockets for a half-smoked cigarette. Nothing. I look around the ground until I find a butt with a few drags on it stamped out beside an unmarked grave. I rip off the meth-breath filter and smoke it down until the skin under my nails burns. Without a drink or a line to wash it down, the taste makes me gag. I can feel my stomach working hard to digest the hair I've been chewing on and the thick speed paste. Right as I think I could really use a drink, I realize that, despite the heat, my teeth have begun to chatter.

As I walk on, I start to notice most of the graves are unmarked. I know it's because most people in this town are too poor to waste money on stones for the dead. They would rather spend it on meth and ammo. When I'd come to visit you, we would go cash your welfare checks and buy canned sardines and ravioli because you loved Eyetalian food. Then we'd go to the bingo hall and you'd smoke and holler with your friends and I would use the bingo markers to draw pointillist pictures of happy girls and rainbows out of the disconnected dots and you would pin the trifles on the walls in your mercy apartment with sewing needles. You died without any money, but I inherited other things: a vanity with false teeth in the top drawer, auburn hair, fourteen engagement rings, hazel eyes, a beautiful set of porcelain crochet needles, suicidal tendencies, smoke-stained doilies. I've held on to every piece, piecing them back together, brushing them, polishing them, investigating how you came to have them, trying to find meaning behind everything, as if life were like a ghost story, and as soon as I brought justice to your death, you could finally be set free.

But I can't find you, and the sun is taking its toll. Under my asthmatic wheeze I can hear my heart murmuring. Like so many times before, I find myself wishing I believed in old-time religion, because my bargaining with God feels meaningless. *Please, whoever, let me live and I swear this time I really will quit doing all the drugs. Or at least not mix them. On weekdays.* I haven't slept more than four hours in—I don't know how long. The anxiety of my relationship with the professor, my family, and the speed have been keeping me up most nights. My heart rate is fucked. I can feel it throbbing under my breast pocket, and I try to hold it in my chest cavity with my hand because it feels like it will jump right out of my meager skin and bones. If I don't want to die out here before finding you, I have no choice but to head back to the car and drive a quarter mile down the street to your mother's house and ask her where you are. I call my great-grandmother, Grandmother, because she adopted Mom when you left Menard and your baby. You were fourteen and tired of your brother Jim sneaking into your bedroom at night. You told Grandmother, and she beat the devil out of you and called you a liar. So you got married and left for Austin because, as you told Aunt Betty, if you had to get fucked you'd rather have a say in who'd do it. Forty-five years later, Mom put the pieces together and killed any semblance of love she had left for you. When I asked her why we didn't go to Granny Franny's anymore, she told me how it was all your fault for leaving her there with Jim and Grandmother, who continued to turn a blind eye until the day Jim fell down a well and broke his neck, and when she had finally confronted you on the advice of her therapist, you couldn't apologize. You blamed it on Jim. So I'd learned to hate Jim. It was logical. But I loved you, however illogical Mom made it seem after the fact. I've learned that you can't undo a feeling with logic, nor logic with a feeling.

I stare up at Grandmother's three-story plantation house, sagging into its own filth. Everything white has greyed. When I peer through the back door into the kitchen, there are moldy stacks of bills and letters on the table and cobwebs in the window. No one has lived here in a long time. The doors are all locked, but I've lost enough weight to be able to crawl under the house like when I was a kid. I knock down fossilized hornet nests from my old hideaway and sneak my way inside through the trap door, rising up from the ground like the dead.

Everything is as I've expected. My meth head cousins have stolen everything of value and things they were too dumb to know had no value—old TV sets with broken bulbs, my Uncle Dewey's amateur taxidermy, your macramé throw pillows. The only things left are pictures of our dull-eyed, grimacing folk haunting the walls. No one smiles in our family portraits, dating back for two hundred years. I find your postcard picture on the wall from your Rat Pack groupie days, a coy sneer sneaking up one cheek. I pocket it when I hear someone at the door.

"Hello, who's there?"

I peer through the black screen to see who it is. I don't know the person waiting on the porch, but I recognize those meth teeth. I see she has a gun.

"Who are you? What are you doing here?" She coughs on her words so hard I think she'll knock one of the little yellow rocks loose from her shrunken gums. I wonder if she'd try to smoke it.

"I'm Mary's granddaughter. Great-granddaughter. From Austin." I eye the gun. "Do you know where she is?"

"Shit. She hasn't lived here in years."

"Do you know where she is?" I repeat, hoping the words will sink in before she decides to shoot me. I look down at the shotgun, and the woman lowers it as she slowly connects the dots.

"Hey. Aren't you that kid used to come play with my boy, Stuart?"

"I'm not sure."

"Yeah, you were that chubby kid who ate all my Little Debbies." She smiles a little bit. Or at least I think the widening hole in her mouth is a smile. "She's just down the street, at the hospital."

"Hospital?"

"Shit, you know, the old folks' home. She's been there for years. Shit! How do you not know?" She laughs and waits for me to say something. But I have no words for her. I don't want to sit around getting to know her. That's not why I've come. But she has nothing better to do. She almost looks happy to be distracted but I leave just the same. I wave as I drive away but she doesn't wave back.

When I walk inside the senior care building it's nothing like I remembered. I used to volunteer here during the summers, but death means nothing to children and I was blind to the corroding walls, ceilings, and faces. A woman in Garfield scrubs takes me to a small, yellow room with vinyl tulip curtains. There are plastic flowers everywhere.

"Mary, there's someone here to see you!" The nurse is practically singing, her pupils bulging out of her irises. Everyone in this town is doped up. She sashays away and I almost don't recognize the old woman staring back at me with green veins bulging from thin, translucent skin, white-white wiry hair sticking up in every direction from her shrunken head, her once clear, sky-blue eyes milky and crusted. Grandmother looks much older than I remember. I realize she is the oldest person I've ever seen.

"Hi, Grandmother," I stammer. "It's me." I haven't seen her since my family history lesson. When my mother found my stash of drugs and had thrown them into the bottom of the trashcan, soaking up the rotting juices, and I'd dived in after them since I knew they'd be fine, I just needed to dry them out and they'd be fine, the drugs would still work even if it was gross, how she'd dragged me out by my hair and I just let her rip it out, I just kept kicking and screaming until my mother slapped me hard across the face, loosened a tooth that eventually fell out into the toilet after another rough night.

"You're just like your Granny Franny! You're a selfish bitch! You don't care how what you do affects me!"

I want to tell my grandmother she's a bitch, a cunt, an accomplice to rape, a matriarch of incest and death. But she reaches out for my hand and I hold the leathery glove of twisted bones in mine, noting their resemblance to my own knotted knuckles. She looks up in my direction with opaque vagueness, clouds in her eyes and tears streaming down her face. She is sobbing, trying to tell me how she thought she'd never see me again. She tries to ask about my mom and sister but she is sobbing too hard, choking on an old, yellowed Kleenex that she's been holding on to for what must be days. I don't know how to ask her what I came to ask, don't know how to tell her I'd rather visit a dead woman's grave than her. She never did anything to me directly. But she made it damn near impossible for anyone in my family to trust each other, to really love each other. She begs me to take her to her house. She can't go without a chaperone and no one has been by to take her away from this place in months. The dopey nurse is watching our melodrama. I don't blame her. Nothing exciting ever happens in this town. I can't say no. It takes forty minutes to walk her from the street to the house, her gun-toting neighbor watching us from a lawn chair in her driveway all the while. When I get Grandmother inside, she sits down in her old chair and looks around trying to see the room through her cataracts. She can't see what they've done to her beautiful house. Not telling her is the only kindness I can think of to offer her. She tells me to take whatever I want. I don't want any more damning inheritance from this place so I just take a few of your photos down from the walls, revealing patches of the wallpaper's original fleur-de-lis pattern. I always thought it was hilarious how your family tried to convince itself that it was French when they couldn't trace their lines back further than Georgia. An entire lineage based on self-deceit. I sit down and watch Grandmother stroke the worn parts of her chair, humming and muttering to herself.

"This is where your granny died. Doped out on pills. I found her here the night before. I thought I should just let her. . . sleep it off."

I want to scream at her, you dumb bitch, you drove her to the pills and you couldn't be bothered to call 911 when she ODs? But I don't. I need her to tell me what I came to find out.

"Where was she buried?" I ask through clenched teeth. "Eh?"

I speak slower than my heart wants me to. "Where was Granny buried?"

"I don't know. I didn't go. I just. . . couldn't. . . go."

I shake my head but she doesn't see. She doesn't see anything. Part of me wants to pop another little orange pill and get out of here as fast as I can, but my heart is already racing and I realize if I OD out here I'm as good as dead.

"Come on, Grandmother. I have to take you back."

I take one last look at the house where every woman in my family lived, lost their innocence, and ran away from. I feel proud to carry the torch for them. I want to do better, for all of us. On the way out, I pull the faded prescription bottle from my breast pocket, running my fingers over the childproof cap. I empty my stash of pills on the curb, and when I look back that nosey meth bitch is shoving some into her pocket and a fistful into her mouth.

I get Grandmother back into her deathbed and kiss her goodbye. It pains me somewhat to know she will die alone, but I can't interfere with justice. There are a few bluebonnets left on the floor of my car that have wilted in the heat. Not even our state flower can thrive here once it's been plucked. What hope was there for us?

I walk to the tree from my dreams and arrange the flowers into your initials. I tell you goodbye, knowing I won't be back. There is nothing so drought resistant as forgiveness. I got what I came for. In the end, you wouldn't even have your bones chained to a grave. I wonder if you finally feel free. As free as I feel now.

Ignite

There is nothing left in the room but an incense stick. I asked him if I could have it after it had burned halfway down. That's how long it took for me to be sure, to follow the smoke signals of memory, to remember the smell of a woman now only bones and a fistful of hair combed back by the false teeth that fell back in her head when the muscles of her soft smoker's mouth decomposed in her unmarked grave.

He was reluctant to give me anything, afraid I would take it the wrong way, but I grabbed it, held on to it in front of me like a broken spear, and he didn't take it from my hand. I slipped it into the breast pocket of my faux leather coat, the shoulders tattered into moth wing shapes from the months of him pushing me out of his apartment, in his wicked half-embrace, after he'd already come inside of me enough times for it to not be fun for him anymore, which, I'll tell you, was seven, before running down those pastel Excelsior hills that I knew I'd never see again.

His room was like he was, full of himself, but, for whatever reason, he had an old tin box of incense, hundreds of them crumbling to a delicious, fragrant powder, sage-grey hues of dust that housed the bones of my grandmother's memory. Her belongings had scattered in the wind when she'd died. I'd collected the pieces too heavy to blow away: golden rings and brass picture frames with old cardboard backings held together with rusted staples and yellow tape. But her face was different in pictures, and the glass didn't smell like her anymore.

I asked him where he'd found the bundle of my grandmother's incense, and I could tell by the silence falling from his eyes that he was guilty. I knew then that the months we'd spent together in that room getting to know how each of us transformed the space of a place were all leading up to this confession at the altar. I let him show me out, and when I was sure he was no longer looking after me I ran as fast as I could until I was out of breath. Only then did I inhale the floral dust into the deepest part of myself, choking on jasmine, ivy, a scent as immense as a body.

Home in my small shadow of a room, I placed the incense on my bookshelf, but the books were old and molding with a sour yellow smell. I brought the incense to my lips and breathed, its scent already fainter, coalescing with the diseased pages. The books had to go, and I left them spine up outside the door where they vanished one by one. My porous, cotton-dry clothes, too, seemed to be absorbing the smell of the flowers, polluting them with their factory dust and cheap fabric softener, so I threw each garment, piece by piece, out the window, where baby pigeons hatched from the pockets. But then there was the hot breath of night in the city, the yeasty thirst of sunlight, and what else? The furniture went down the window well, I nailed the windows shut. Even the fruit flies that refused to leave, with their sweet eggy breath, had to be crushed under my nails, their sweet metallic smelling blood washed down the drain, before I noticed the mineral-logged water, the chlorinated smell of it, so I turned off the water to preserve the fragrant stick. I boarded up the door. I shut my mouth. Now it's just my incense stick and me. I'd light it but for my fear of the smell of the sulfurous match. So I sit and stare, waiting for it to ignite.

Teeth

I tried to keep you. When love's niceties failed, I tried witchcraft. I spat in your drinks, kept a lock of your beard in my pocket, lit virgin candles, learned a little Latin, made love to you on my period (*imbubino*), put baby teeth underneath your pillow.

Now you never leave my side.

But all I see when you smile at me is a mouthful of baby teeth.

With Our Heads Bowed

She waits for the sound of her father's gun to strike the cedar table. The ribs of his chair expand for breath as he burdens them with his immense weight. He is counting the money that he carries, that makes every night dangerous. The porcelain lid of their earthen jar scrapes open and shut as he hides the wad of green paper under the white peels of garlic. She blows out her candles and fans the smoke before sliding under the covers. She sucks on the damp tassels of her blanket out of habit. The threads have been made sweet over the years from her continuous sucking on them in the moments spent waiting for her father, when the burden of her life was no longer hers and she could relax, sleep. She never knows if this is the night the men her father carries a gun for will come for what's in their jar. Years have gone by without any shots but the scars on her father's arms, torso, and face are as ugly as ever.

She hears him climbing the stairs, coming towards her room. The house creaks as if still surprised by the heavy steps of its owner. He opens her door and peers inside, his dark eyes spitting up the amber light of the oil lamp in his hand.

He sees the half moon of her eyes peeking at him through the dark. "What are you doing up?"

Her other eye, invited, opens. "No tengo sueño, Papa. I can't sleep."

"A girl is never too old to ask her father to tell her a story," he whispers. She smiles and sits up. He smiles too, the left side of his face barely lifting from the wound that has left it paralyzed. He walks to the corner of the room, where his wooden guitar leans against the wall. He grabs the neck and strums a chord with his thick, agile fingers, the nylons thrashing back and forth with tremendous speed. He adjusts the wooden knobs, and each string goes taut as an anxious nerve. He bows his head before he sings, as he always does. It is something she has always noticed but has never mentioned. She merely bows hers and listens.

He sings her the same stories he has always sung, about Los Malos, a group of boys so hateful they beat an old bruja one night just to keep warm. When the woman came to, she turned them into venomous snakes with a terrible thirst for wood. When they struck the passing wagon wheels with their parched fangs, the wood swelled and burst in their mouths. They lost their fangs and slowly starved as the termites left in their throats ate them from the inside out.

He sings to her of a man who was born stiff as a sand dollar, his skeleton made of five long bones. One day the man came across the devil, who broke all the man's bones, *here and there*, her father would always sing, giving him more joints than a scorpion. He became such a beautiful dancer that the most beautiful woman in the village fell in love with him. But when her husband found them together he broke his wife's neck, and the man's heart turned to sand.

He sings to her of the winter he fell in love with her mother. It was the year that the red mountains fell and the cold winds from the north blew in. It became so frigid that when he tried to tell her he loved her, his words froze in his mouth and fell to the ice-covered ground, entombed all winter by the falling snow. In the spring, a flower whispered the words at her funeral.

———

She lifts her head, roused by the wooden frame of the house adjusting to the hollowness her father has left. He does not come back that night, nor the next. The guitar collects dust between the strings, and the jar is empty save a few leaves of garlic. She asks the neighbors if they've seen her father but they all shake their heads. She goes into the market and asks the owner and the man selling garlic. They tell her no, they have not seen her father. She is given a braid of garlic and told not to worry. She does. She asks the men sweating on the porches drinking cerveza if they have seen her father. No, they tell her. As she walks away some of them whistle as if nothing were wrong. She goes home, spices corn for dinner, takes the garlic braid to bed. She cannot sleep, and her covers are too short. The tassels on her woven blanket tickle the hairs on her legs and keep her awake. She peels the garlic clove by clove in her sleep as if it were the rosary.

In the dark she tries to recite her father's stories but the words disappear into the flatness of the strings, the sharpness of her voice. She is afraid of what waits for her outside of her bedroom. She tries to recall a happy story to illuminate her room, to give her the courage to move. But there are none. Her father never believed in happy endings. She has never felt so childish for believing he'd been saving one for her. She walks downstairs, gets the jar, and begins to whisper words into the empty vessel, filling it with her own.

Skinlace

"There's a cock-eyed woman with a rose-colored shadow and a gluttonous thirst for blood. She comes out at night, the blood is bled, and she webs like a spider the dead man's head!"

Sarah Jane squeals and grabs my hand. Everyone in Rigantana has heard the same tale since birth and believes it to be true until death. It is a tale that belongs to moonless nights and the small hours of autumn, and Niles Ray tells it best. He knows just when to capstone his voice and leap into the audience, sauntering hunchbacked, growling through his teeth like a mad cat. He always knows who the screamers are, and tonight there are plenty, for this is the first time we've ever dared to meet under the old hanging tree on Slaughter Lane, where Temperance Calloway swears on her mother's grave she once saw the old witch slither up the trunk.

"Cut it out Niles!" I tell him, loosening my hand from Sarah Jane's boney grip.

Niles smiles his wicked Ray brothers' grin at us, his freckled lips disappearing into the pink of his mouth. He crouches down in front of Sarah Jane, his wicked, yellow eyes looking up into the treetops.

"Shh. You wouldn't want Skinlace to hear you hollering like that, would you? She'll gobble the voice right out of your throat!" His lips fold back over his teeth and he snaps them down one, two, three times. Sarah Jane squeals and the other kids snicker, even though they are afraid, too.

"You know, someday someone is going to scare you, Niles Ray!" I grab Sarah Jane's hand and pull her back home towards the orphanage. Niles pitches rocks and sticks and whatever he can at our backs as we run, singing after us, "Skiiinlace, gonna cut your face, Skiiinlace won't leave a trace. . ."

The next morning, Ms. Caslon looks at the empty desk and asks the class if anyone has seen Niles Ray. Tabitha Hudd points her wart-pocked finger out the window. Everyone looks outside and chair after chair cracks the floor as we try to get a closer look. We are pressing our noses against the cold panes, fogging up the glass. The hoop swing in the courtyard spins in the wind, webbed with a bloody rope of skin. A red robin sits perched upon the strung out freckled lips, pecking at the human twine, gathering the textile flesh for its nest. Ms. Caslon collapses onto the floor. The lesson is over. On the way out, we look at each other and nod our heads, our lips mouthing the hollow word we are too afraid to say out loud. Skinlace.

I wake at midnight and hear the throaty grumble of a cat and feel tears waxing hot on my face. They are the tears of that witch, Skinlace. Even in the dark of my rose-window room, I recognize the hook of her nose and her coral shadow looming on my floorboards. She has a glow all her own. It's the first time I've ever seen a witch, and even though she's not cock-eyed, I'm scared. She hovers over me, bathing my face with her blood-logged tears. Our eyes lock and I wait. She massages the sticky paste into my face, neck, and chest.

"Are you here to kill me?" I hear myself ask. Skinlace leans in close. She is older than I am, but not by much. She rubs a handful of my hair into a knot, like the ones framing her luminous face, and I think she is trying to talk with her hands, the way I do sometimes even though Ms. Caslon says it isn't lady-like. My eyes cannot keep still as her wing-like hands weave kaleidoscope patterns in the shadows with the strands of hair she's taken. I blink and she is gone.

Skinlace only comes out at night. When she comes to my room, I know she is there before I open my eyes because I can smell her. She smells like metal after the rain: cold, slick, rust. Her skin is as cold and transparent as Christmas snow. Once, I touched her cheek and the skin cracked faster than the Crum when Sarah Jane tried to run across the frozen lake. When you look at her, all you see at first are the veins and the wrinkles and the tangles, but there is also something beautiful. She holds my gaze and her perpetual lack of expression is comforting in its honesty. I don't remember my mother and father, but if they were alive maybe they'd have come running to me hollering myself hoarse the way Skinlace has. I try to tell her all of this as we walk in the moonlight, but she is restless, and before I can say, I love you, she is nose to the ground, hunting for truffles. She gives each one to me.

On Halloween the road is filled with portly monsters, sugar-faced skeletons, and modest beasts of all creeds. Paper ghosts flutter down from every tree lining the path except for the old hanging tree on Slaughter Lane. Skinlace has hung apples, walnuts, snail tails, junebug shells, feathers, hen's teeth, and marigold heads from the lowest branches of her home. No one has gone back since we found Niles Ray but I'm not afraid. I collect all the apples and walnuts that will fit in the folds of my skirt. The apples are sweeter than any I've ever tasted and the walnuts are buttery and rich. I don't take the snail tails, junebug shells, feathers, hen's teeth, or marigold heads, but when I wake the next morning there is a mayday crown on my pillow woven with the trinkets. When I wear it to the breakfast table, Governess Mallory shrieks in disgust and snatches the wreath off my head. The snail tails and junebug shells crumble through her fingers and fall into my watery bowl of oatmeal. She rolls up her sleeves and adjusts her tight silver bun and sends me out back to find a switch for my chastening. The next day there is another bloody web in the courtyard and Skinlace gives me the most beautiful corn doll with a thick head of pearly, silver hair.

Skinlace takes to the wind like bible paper. She teaches me how to fly in my dreams, and I explore the fantastic labyrinth of the world with such weightlessness that when I awake it is with a heavy heart that I find myself earthbound. I stretch out my arms and jump, but when I open my eyes I'm still standing on flat feet. Skinlace must have seen the shadows of heartache in my face when she floated out of reach, for she has kept to the ground ever since.

Skinlace takes me to the river, and we hunt for salamanders under the rocks. I learn that salamander heads glow in the dark. Skinlace tells me it's because they are magic, that a salamander's spirit is strong enough to grow back the missing pieces of itself. She bites the tail off the one I catch and tells me to take it home. She says that when the tail grows back I will be able to walk through fire. After two weeks living in the cracks of my moldy bedroom walls, the salamander's tail does grow back, but I am too afraid to face the flames. I open the window and wait for it to leave, but it stays.

Skinlace tells me that she had dreamed of me long before I was born, and this is how she knows I'm hers.

Since the death of Governess Mallory, Cotton Withers has taken on the charisma of a bloodhound. Rigantana has become a whisper of a town amidst all the accusations of foul play and deviltry. No one talks to anyone, no one goes anywhere, everyone is suspect until that eager know-it-all, Temperance Calloway, comes forward and tells everyone in Sunday service where to find the murderess witch. I run to the woods with the hound on my heels. I hesitate before calling her name. I've never thought of Skinlace existing in the hours of daylight until now. She does not answer. I yell until my voice cracks but the only one who answers my calls is Minister Withers. He calls me a traitor, a witch, and has the parishioners bind me to the tree.

When the Sun goes down, the town is foaming at the mouth. They erect a log pyramid around the tree and me, eager to burn both. When I hear the scratch of a match on sandpaper, I close my eyes. I feel tears running down my face, as the sweet birch starts to smoke. I hear the throaty grumble of a cat and a long, desperate scream. Sarah Jane has been watching quietly, held back by the others, but now she is pulling away, crawling backwards. I feel Skinlace slither down my side. "I'm not afraid," I tell her. "Fly away," I beg her. "I'm not afraid." I open my eyes, realizing that what I've said is the truth. Skinlace steps into the flames, her head glowing brighter than the salamanders'.

The black shadows on the ground make no sound once overcome by her coral shadow. They disappear into the flickering light, limb by limb. The tree is all flame and the ropes holding me back burn to ash. I walk through the fire and watch the flames spit into the stars. As the tree collapses onto its ashen base, a horde of old bones fall from the topmost branches into the pyre. The embers erupt under the weight of the remains before snowing down onto my skin. Skinlace comes to my side, a line of blood dripping down her throat, Minister Withers' scalp twisted in her long, knitting fingers. We stare at the ashes of what was her home. I tell her not to cry, that we will find a new one.

This is no dream, and this is how I know I am hers.

Solid

He boasted of never having broken a bone. He was solid. He'd never gotten a cavity, never took sick, never fallen in love.

She thinks of this as she chops through limestone and dirt. Indian rock, her father called it, though it is only now that she thinks to ask why. The shovel does little but spark the flint. She digs and digs until she no longer recognizes her own hands, so thick with blood. She has to stop often and remove the skeletal fragments of limestone. Thinner pieces crumble easily in her hands, and she feels as if she has stumbled upon some great, absolving secret: there had never been any solid ground for them to stand on. She kicks him into the hole. His blood starts to fill it.

In the end, she can't bring herself to sink the big toe. When the body is found in the spring, she is questioned, shown the remains. But she knows this decomposed thing is not him. She had put her ear to the ground and listened to it take him. She had felt it. The earth under her feet had never been so solid.

Taken

She allows herself to be taken in the hopes of escaping her own personal landscape. No one told her how easy it was to see promise in a stranger's eyes, nor how hard it was to rot in a bad marriage. Her taker's neck is wrapped in a bandana the color of milk-logged sand. When he enters the house he tracks red dust clouds onto the sun-bleached floorboards. He leaves no footprints, only violent lines and circles. She offers him coffee, cream, molasses. He tells her he takes it black and that she can bring a few of her things if she'd like. She goes to the next room where she and her husband have slept next to each other since the day she turned seventeen. She looks around and realizes she has nothing to pack. Everything is wooden, heavy, nailed to the walls. Eventually she decides to bring a block of thyme soap wrapped in a leather strap, two fingers wide, that has held a loose board to the bedside table that her husband once threw at her when he found a finger-shaped bruise on her thigh. If it turns for the worse, she can always hang herself, she thinks, staring at her bundle. She thinks about leaving a note. But there is no ink, and there are no words.

She feigns resistance, like a lady. The day seems right for a taking, the sky opaque as the gritty innards of a desert moth. In three days time, she no longer recognizes the land. Mountains rise from the dermis of the earth, blemishing the view, penetrating the sky. Come night, the clusters of stars offer some form of familiarity, but she begins to see her husbands face in the open jaws of black clouds. The bandit moves fast, straight, as if he knows where he's going, as if he knows where her husband is not. She thinks to tell him her husband will not come for them, will not leave his mother's grave. Where they arrive, the dirt is hard, a thin cake over deep rock. Monolith towers above them, small rock ruins of castles, temples, reduced to piles of stone make her wary of the possibility of survival. Bones sit under piles of rock, dirt, and waste, play peek-a-boo with reptilian faces and crow's feet. She wonders how anyone could be buried here, let alone live here, and yet here she is.

The bandit's brought with them to this deserted juniper grove a knife, a bottle of red wine, cherries, apricots, slices of heirloom tomatoes marinating in apple vinegar and sage, plenty of rope, almond wood, a book of matches, and a book of prose as dog-eared and straight-spined as himself. If he has faltered in asserting his intentions, at least the landscape is captivating.

"The desert has no body."
"We are nobody."

As he builds the fire, she worries about the wind blowing a shiver of hunger across a mountain lion's belly. As he stokes the fire, she worries about being devoured foot first by a misstep on a canyon perch. As he breaks apart the embers, she worries about the red splinter in the pink under her thumb's nail. She has discovered an allergy to juniper and a deep hatred for this plant that has turned on her green thumb.

Before the dark takes them, he takes the knife, holds her hand, brings the blade to her flesh, and slides the splinter out. She is afraid until he presses the spot of blood on her finger to his lips. The only mirror she has is the glass of his opallus eyes, a laurel green radiance within the void of the pallor of his face, always ready to meet hers. As if the scenery means nothing to him. Perhaps she is beautiful, a sight to behold. Perhaps he is only measuring the pulse in her temples, the angle of her gaze, so he can measure the paths that could lead her away from him. Every morning he blindfolds her with his hands, leads her somewhere new. She notices his hands are immaculate, not what she imagined for a kidnapper. His fingers are deft, smooth as the monolith towers he holds her in, as thick at the joints as prickly pear blossoms. Perhaps he has built the scenery around them with those thick square hands, pulled the very rocks from the earth, hammered the blue into the white hot sky above their heads, screaming into their eyes with every knuckle crack of dawn.

From his book he pulls a bouquet of dried flowers. She takes them gingerly, when the look in his eyes tells her he has picked them for her.

The longer they stay, the more they feign ignorance of their origins.

He is a fish full of bones and salt water and baited hooks.

She thinks of colors only in abstractions. Cobalt, indigo, and cerulean landscapes.

Yet evidence of unconscious fears emerge on their faces like the silent white door that opens every day from the horizon before shutting them up in the deep blue night.

They do not stay in one place for long. Each place they discover is haunted in its own way. Cicadas drum in the hollow skeletons of junipers. White lights, bodiless eyes, follow them from dusk till dawn. She wonders if the soft mounds of dirt they pass are dead anthills or graves. He worries she will be bitten by ants or think the dusty dunes at her feet are graves he has dug . Does she not see how clean his hands are? Does she not wonder why he hasn't touched her?

They come to a town as dead as all. A breath of dust blows across the red earth, pinning a dirty, yellowed rebozo to the landscape. It waves, whipping at the air, caught between desert winds and barbed wire. Rock litters the road, the land undeveloping itself. Small, one-story dwellings hug the ground. Some of the ribs of the houses have broken, spilling their hearts before their feet. In the grass, sandy asparagus heads perch above broken stained glass, bottle caps, nails. She cannot get enough of it. She devours the stalks one by one, between her teeth, until finally, the asparagus, too, is gone.

What is it that made them devour the land this way?

With nowhere else to go, they return to their origins.

Everything is final, occurs again and again.

He doesn't know when exactly he lost her. The time went by, and yet alone it seems nothing has happened.

"I thought you died."

She stands knee deep in the salty wash of wine-dark water. She's been looking for a fish full of bones and salt water and baited hooks.

"What is it exactly that you want?" The pupils dilate, an explosion of black ash in the cobalt, indigo, and cerulean landscape.

"One moment more beneath the night with you."

Under Orion's Belt

"Throw on another log," I said. "We'll make it until morning." You bit back the bow of my lips and let me lick the laurel veins underneath your tongue.

You offered my cup, resting on your palm, to Orion, because, "Hey," you said, "let's get the bastard drunk, slip off his belt, and hang the moon by its hallowed neck, so the halo of hereafter never comes. Because we'll never make it till morning, and if we go down, I'm bringing the sky down with us."

Clay

I know something is wrong when Mama Leta calls me from the cell phone. She's had a cell phone for ten years now and never uses it to call anyone. She uses it as a replacement watch, too self-conscious about her plump wrists and liver-spotted hands to draw attention to them with a flashy, silver timepiece, and only answers it one out of one hundred times to say, "I'm almost home. I'll call you back on the landline."

It's been a good morning, so far. The heat wave is finally over, and the water restrictions have been lifted, and the radio Co-op's been playing my favorite music, so I've spent all morning pursuing my shallow pleasure of dancing in the garden in just a t-shirt and underwear while chain-smoking and nursing my shriveled plants back to life. But when I see my mother's cell phone on caller ID, my whole body tenses, mud rising up between my naked toes as they dig into the soft earth.

"It's your Mama Su," Mama Leta tells me through static, while the stream from my hose splashes my chayote. I roll my eyes and turn my attention back to fertilizing my plants with cigarette ash. "What now?" I ask. "Another girlfriend? Another bankruptcy? Another stint in the drunk tank?"

"She's sick. . . Cancer came back. . . I don't know. . . A few weeks if she's lucky, if you can call it that. I just ran into Barbara at Central Market. She was buying flowers. Orchids, if you can believe it..."

I don't know how much time has passed when I finally speak, but my cigarette has gone out and the chayotes have flooded. The thick stalk leans over like a woman getting ready to run.

"Mom?" I ask into the receiver, without really meaning to ask anything. Even though I haven't spoken to Mama Su in three years,

I feel sick for being the kind of person that scoffs at a dying woman.

I hear my mother sigh heavily into the mouthpiece. "I'm sorry, baby. Why don't you come over later? I'm making tortilla soup." Mama Leta's cure for any sorrow is always hot food.

I mumble something about coming over tomorrow for leftovers and hang up before she can tell me day-old caldo is una lástima, a real shame. I chuck the half-smoked cigarette, blotted with lipstick and tar, into the waste bin on top of an empty tube of toothpaste that's been stuck to the bottom with fluoride plaster for months. My ex, Griffen, once told me you can tell everything you need to know about a person by what their tube of toothpaste looks like. Rolled up tight from the bottom means compulsively neat or habitual joint roller. Squeezed right from the top means not very bright. Squeezed from the middle with toothpaste smeared all over it, like mine, means impulsive, anxious, messy. I told him yes, I agreed, toothpaste tubes spoke volumes, but that it was cultural. He rolled his eyes and started keeping his own travel size Crest in my bathroom drawer before he finally took his toothpaste and everything else to another girl's house because, unlike me, "She was easy," which I took to mean a bottom roller. I tried to explain it to him, how Mama Su came from the poorest of trailer trash, which meant my teeth never had a chance. When she was thirty, Mama Su had all her teeth, yellow and black as picnic corn, cracked and pried out piece by piece and replaced with false ones because she never even owned a toothbrush until her mid-twenties. Before Mama Leta came around, Mama Su never took me to the dentist, either. It was the eighties, and she was afraid I'd get AIDS from a dental pick. When the nineties came and people calmed down, even my mother thanks to Mama Leta, I'd already acquired my haphazard toothpaste habits and more cavities than teeth. I've had them filled since then, but every now and then one of the fillings will fall out, and when I look in the mirror and open wide I see how full of holes I really am.

But despite all of the emptiness Mama Su has left in me, part of me wants to make peace with her so I can make peace with myself, to know that unlike her drug-addled wife-and-child-abandoning ass, I don't run away from my problems. I call Mama Su on the drive over and her newest girlfriend answers. I know Barbara's not happy to hear from me, but due to the circumstances she's at least willing to fake it, to cushion her cold, short words with extra consonants and vowels.

"Hi, Barbara," I say.

"Oh, hiii."

"Listen, is it alright if I come see y'all?"

"Mmm, of course."

"Great, could you ask her if she wants me to bring anything? Smokes and soda? Ok. I'm on my way."

"Ok huuun. Drive saaafe."

The air conditioning in the corner store is out again, and the whole place smells like a bad hotdog, but I still spend twenty minutes contemplating the ingredients of an off-brand bag of Cheetos, counting the carcinogens. I wonder how many bags of these I've had over my lifetime and reckon it's in the hundreds. I try to remember the last time I went in for a checkup, and start to give my breasts a self-exam in the middle of the aisle. A young, suspicious looking clerk with acne and bushy raised eyebrows calls out, "Can I help you ma'am?" I realize it's the first time anyone's ever called me "ma'am," and I know then that I'm too old to be still running away from my mother. I want to cry. I look at my disembodied image in the security monitor and hold my breath, waiting to see if the girl on screen keeps it together.

"Pack of Marlboro Reds and a Big Gulp," she croaks. "Credit. Thanks."

It takes me half an hour to drive down South First Street, and when I sip the Coke at the last stoplight before Barbara and Mama Su's, it's watered down enough to taste like diet, just the way she likes it, or I should say, used to. I'm not sure anymore. I wonder if she's changed much in the three years since I've seen her. It's always the little things that people seem to change—a taste for red peppers or onions, new piercings and faded tattoos, a love for poetry, bangs, lovers. If I hadn't given up on Mama Su long ago, I'd hope that some things about her would have changed other than her taste buds.

There's never any street parking in the crowded little alley in front of the row of duplexes, so I pull as far into the half driveway as I can without running Mama Su over. She's sitting in an old lawn chair that looks like it's about had it. She's gotten fat, but it suits her okay. She isn't all skin and clavicle, red-eyed from her body's battle with uppers and downers and in-betweeners like I remember. She looks like she's been taking care of herself, but I know this just means she's done well in delegating the task.

"Hey, kiddo." She hoists herself up on a cane, silver and crooked as my fillings. "You look good."

"You too."

"Ah, I look like shit. I've gotten terribly, terribly fat from all the pills they've got me taking. Sit down. Unless you got somewhere to be?"

"No. I'm right where I need to be." I try to say this as accusingly as I can, but somehow it comes out as after-school special. I wince. As usual, Mama Su is too worried about what she needs to notice what I do.

"Hey, you got the Reds," she says holding out a withered pouch of hand bones. "You remembered."

"Ma, you've been smoking those awful cowboy cancer sticks my whole life." I flinch at the word. "Can I have one?" I ask, changing the subject.

"Sure, kid, sure." She taps the pack against her palm weakly and even though she's been smoking since '71, fumbles with the plastic wrap like it's her first time.

She picks up one of her prescription bottles off the side table. Someone's already taken the top off for her. "Want one?"

"I'm okay, thanks." She chases down the pills with the Coke, and the Coke with a cigarette. We sit there sizing each other up, listening to an old blues record on my old portable record player, one of the many things she's stolen from me that we both pretend was hers all along to spare each other's feelings. But looking at it now, I can't help but tap the ash on my cigarette so hard that the ember spills out of the paper.

"How's Barbara?" I ask flatly, trying to seem as uninterested as possible.

"Fine. How's school? Still working on your MF-"

"A. MFA. Yeah."

"Good, good. Still working on your novel?"

"I finished it. You know that." And even though I look away, I know she's rolling her eyes at me.

"Well, I'm sure you made some changes since then. I wish you'd let me read it again sometime before—"

"Sure," I blurt out, not wanting her to finish the sentence. "I'll bring it over sometime." I know that I won't and hate that she's made me as big of a liar as she is.

"Sure," she says looking at me through silted eyes. "Sure you will." The record ends and the needle pulsates in tempo with the blood still pumping hot in my ears from the word, "changes." And then, as if on cue, a guy in his twenties emerges from inside Mama Su's. I wonder if he might be some son of Barbara's that she never mentioned, but no, she hates kids, even the grown-up ones like me. It seems unlikely that two old lesbians would have such a young stud for a gardener or housekeeper, and he looks too rough around the edges to be a nurse. He's clad in denim in every shade of blue and bleach-speckled sneakers, a pouch of tobacco sticking out of his back pocket. He's handsome, tall and thick-legged, with a strong jaw, crystal-blue eyes, and that hair—you never can tell if it's dark blonde or light brown— finger- combed behind his ears, and John Lennon glasses.

"Whatcha feel like now, Susie Q?" he asks.

"Put on some Stevie Ray, will ya?" she says, perking up.

"I could've guessed," he says winking at her. Then as if just realizing they're not alone, he stops and looks at me. I mean, really looks at me, with an unapologetic intensity that makes me forget to breathe. At first I'm put off by his brazen gaze, but immediately fall for the crow's feet framing the bluest eyes I've ever seen. He's looking at me with such gravity that I actually feel myself being pulled towards him. He smiles and finally breaks his stare to sift through Mama Su's milk crate of albums. He chicken-heads to the first few bars of "Southern Blues" before unfurling the tobacco pouch from his pocket.

"Smoke, Susie Q?" And although he's speaking to my mother, he's already sneaking more glances at me.

"I'm alright. Lo brought me some."

"Lo?"

"'Lo and behold,'" my mother says, laughing at her old joke. She tamps out another cigarette and waves casually to the guy. "This is Clay. He lives next door. He's been helping out around here when Barbara's at work."

"Hey," he says to me. The gravity of his gaze pulls me to the edge of my seat. I nod, my tongue fit tightly between my front teeth to keep me from licking my lips obscenely at the most attractive person I've ever seen. He finally looks away to light Mama Su's cigarette. I watch him with my mother. He's good with her. He counts out her pills, lights her cigarettes, adjusts her chair when the sun moves over the trees and into her eyes. Halfway through her third Marlboro, my mother's eyes close, her mouth hanging halfway open letting out slow, deep, smoky breaths. Clay takes the cigarette dangling between her lips and takes a long drag off of it. They appear to be close but I don't hold it against him. He probably doesn't know her that well. But I'm barely thinking of my mother or her sickness anymore. I'm trying to figure this Clay guy out. He is staring at me again in his fierce, quiet way.

"What?" I finally ask, wanting to engage him in conversation. He smiles from lip to eye, his crow's feet winking at me.

"Nothing. Just looking."

I sit down in the grass and point to his vest pocket. "I'll take one of those." He sits next to me and pulls a paper from the packet.

"I'll roll it," I offer. He nods his head, as if pleasantly surprised. It's been a long time since anyone found anything pleasant about my behavior, but Clay makes me feel as if I should take a bow. After the smoke is rolled, I put it in my mouth and I start to pat down my pockets, but before I find my Bic, he's lighting my cigarette. Despite his classic noir behavior and crow's feet, there is something young and wild about the way he's looking at me.

"How old are you?" I ask.

"Twenty-two."

"Jesus. You're just a kid!" He laughs at this and takes a long thoughtful drag.

"'Just a kid,' she says."

"Oh, God. Did you just narrate me? Don't tell me you're a writer." He grins before confessing, "A poet. Some stories, too. Susie Q tells me you're working on a novel? What's it about?"

My spine tenses into an unnatural arc at the mention of my mother and my novel.

I look away and let the smoke ooze from the corners of my frown.

"Clay. That's an interesting name," I say, quickly changing the subject. "Your parents named you after dirt."

"Actually, they named me after my uncle. He died five weeks before I was born. Shot in Chicago by some gang member or something. They never caught the guy who shot him." I blink stupidly, the sudden intimacy washing over me like coarse sand.

"That's horrible," I stammer.

"Yeah," he says, his brows knitting together as if it were the first time he'd really considered it. "It is. I mean, his parents naming him after dirt and all." He winks at me, and I can't help but laugh at his awful joke.

Ma grumbles in her sleep, "Horrible."

Clay smiles at me. "She's pretty cool, your old lady. I mean, she's had an interesting life. She's been kind of like a mother to me since I moved here." Suddenly I want to slap him. But how do I tell a stranger about my mother's brother sexually assaulting her and my grandmother never believing her daughter, letting it go on and on until my mother married the first boy she could so she could get out of there? How she'd gotten pregnant with me at fourteen then left me at her mother's house until I was seven, with her brother, while she went off with her first girlfriend to live her "interesting life." The only person I'd ever told before was Griffen, and even then it was only after things had ended, as a way of trying to get him to realize why I'd been such a mess, to pardon me and take me back. It hadn't worked, and of all the things I regret in life, telling someone something so devastatingly personal only to be immediately rejected was at the top of my list.

"She's dying, you know," I say bluntly.

"Yeah." He looks at me like he's waiting for me to say something else. I sit, not saying anything, and the longer I look at him the more I like what I see.

"You want a drink?" I ask.

"Yeah." It was all "yeah" with him, which I liked. I wanted him to stay with me. I wanted to study his face, the color of his eyes, the topography of those crow's feet. I looked at my mother, half asleep. Then I remember the last time I saw her, how I'd found a squished spider on the first page of the manuscript I'd shown her sticking out of the garbage, and how she'd said that word today, "changes."

"Let's go," I say, fishing my car keys out of my jeans. Clay gets up and kisses my mother on her forehead. She squints one eye open.

"You kids have a nice time."

At the bar, Clay orders a cheap whiskey on the rocks. I order the same. I want to taste what he tastes, and I even pick a seat at the bar in front of a Heineken mirror so I can see everything he sees. We are the only people sitting at the bar. There are fruit flies drowning in the cherry bowl, dizzy with desire. The bored bartender is feeding singles from the tip jar into the jukebox. A minute later, Roy Orbison's "Only the Lonely" is playing. The bartender looks over and winks at us. "What a dick," I say as he walks away, but when I look to Clay for reassurance he's back to staring at me. We sit in silence and size each other up.

"What's the oldest woman you've ever slept with?" I blurt out. I can tell he's holding back laughter.

"Twenty-six."

"That's not old!" I say too loudly. I sip more whiskey. Maybe I can play it off if I seem drunk.

"How old are you?" he asks.

I think of lying about my age, then decide against doing something I've heard Mama Su do a million times. "Twenty-seven. If I was worth a damn as an artist, this is the year I'd kill myself. You know, like Kurt Cobain, Amy Winehouse, Janis Jop—"

"Don't do that," he says.

"Why not?"

His eyes break away from me, and he looks down at his hands, his fingers fumbling with his glass. "Because I don't want you to."

I sit back and take in the words. It's the nicest thing anyone's ever said to me. I remember the last fight I ever picked with Griffen, over something so stupid that no matter how many times I replay the night in my head, our argument always starts differently, with me being too mean or too needy in some different way to get him to notice me, to urge him to the passion I felt for him every moment I breathed, but he only showed at the culmination of a nasty fight. He was chill, forgiving, everything I wasn't. I loved those things about him, and the more we fought the more he'd forgive me, and the more he forgave me the more I felt that he loved me. But that night, when I'd finally stripped away his last lick of patience and said the meanest, most personal things about him I could think of, he'd looked at me, his reddened eyes quivering with hate. "Go kill yourself," he'd said. "Seriously, Lola. You should just go kill yourself." When enough time had passed without hearing from him, I realized he really didn't care if I'd actually killed myself. For all he knew during those weeks, I could've been dead. I couldn't bear to think that I was so awful that someone would actively wish for my death. I hadn't dated anyone since then, afraid that if I drove another person to feel the same way, I would just have to go through with it.

After three more rounds of Chivas Regal and lustful gazes, I follow Clay home. When we get to his door he catcalls me, clucking his tongue and calling, "here, kitty-kitty." I turn around and pretend to wiggle my tail before dashing into the street and yowling. We are laughing like kids, half-screaming. Some neighbor calls from a window for us to shut up and it sets us off even more. "Come here," he says, holding out his hand for me. It's all I want to do. He leads me into his apartment, and while he puts on my favorite Nirvana album I look at his sticky countertops, his acrylic glasses, the clothes piling up three feet from the hamper. It reminds me of the boys I dated when I was his age, and after being called "ma'am" in the corner store, it's nice to feel young again. We make out until even the walls are sweating. His hair falls down, greasy and sweaty as Kurt Cobain's across my face, and I pull him closer, trying to absorb the essence of his body odor. It smells of vinegar, dead roses, cigarettes, and whiskey. I lick his face and let the sour sweat pucker my whole body into a quiver so rapturous, it's almost spiritual. Finally I take off his shirt, unbuckle his pants and we are like spiders, crawling over furniture, sticky countertops, our limbs wrapping around each other's bodies. The whole time he never takes his eyes off me.

Over the next few weeks, I visit Mama Su daily knowing that I'll see Clay and that he'll find some new way to make me feel good. He is always happy to see me, always ready to lead me away by the hand to some whiskey bar or dark corner. Clay talks mostly about himself, which is fine with me. I'm not interested in hashing out the details of my life, what growing up with Mama Su was like, how I'm feeling while the cancer grows inside of her. Instead I listen to Clay's stories, pin his poems on the wall, fall in love with him. Everything he tells me about himself pushes Mama Su further into the back of my mind. He shows me his sister's artwork, talks about his cigarette-sneaking mother who died of pneumonia rather than kick the habit, and his father, who preached of love and gun control before he finally went mad and hung himself after his brother Clay was killed. After he tells me about his father, Clay finally stops smiling, winking, staring. I take his face in my hands and pull him as close to me as alchemy will allow. I let him lie there while I listen to our heartbeats fall in sync.

"I want to show you something," he finally says. I follow him into his small closet, the dim bulb flickering brighter until it burns a bright white halo above our heads. He opens a cedar chest and pulls out a long-sleeved, yellow, flannel shirt. He cradles it in his arms in a way I would only think to do for a small animal or infant. "I've never shown anyone this," he says. He unfolds it and hangs it out in front of him. "This was my dad's shirt. Before that it was my uncle's. And before that—it was Kurt Cobain's." I can tell by looking at it that it's never been washed. I can smell the Seattle air, the cold, slick rainwater, unwashed hair, heroin. He's staring at it, caressing the fabric with his thumbs. He tries to hand me the shirt, and I step back into the wall.

"You don't think it's bad luck? I mean, me being twenty-seven and all? What if it's, I don't know, cursed? I mean, everyone who's owned it—" I stop myself from saying, "killed themselves." He pulls the shirt back to his chest and looks down at it as if calculating the risk.

"Well, how about you wear it, but it's still mine. That way, if it has any bad luck, it falls on me." He lifts my chin up and kisses me hard on the mouth. "Come on. Take it. I won't let anything bad happen to you, Lo." And the way he says it so matter-of-factly, I believe him. I peel my t-shirt off, put on the flannel, and roll up the too-long sleeves, exposing the goose bumps raising up and down my arms. I can't believe I'm wearing Clay's Kurt Cobain shirt, something that now has belonged to two of the men I've loved most in my life. To prolong the magic, we put on Clay's "In Utero" album and pop Mama Su's opiates in her driveway. Mama Su and Barbara come out with margaritas and give the whole nineties grunge scene we've recreated a try. Everyone is laughing, delirious from the pills and sun, dreamy laughter causing the neighbors to peek at us through their venetian blinds, shaking their heads at us before snapping them shut.

The next morning I go to Clay's, but he isn't there. He's next door, with my mother. Mama Su can't get out of bed. She says her head is too heavy to lift on her own, and she can't swallow her pills. Clay grinds them down in the mortar and rubs the medicine on her gums, her tongue, the pockets of her thumbs. The intimacy of it frightens me. I wait for Mama Su to wave him away, to ask for me, to tell him, "Let Lola do it," but she doesn't and I'm glad. I don't want to face her death, to hold its hand. But Clay does hold her hands and sings her her favorite songs. He blesses her body with sage and incense and gives her whatever she wants. A week later she is throwing up the caldo Mama Leta had me bring over everywhere, tears and vomit plastered to her chin, weighing down her hair. Clay unflinchingly changes my mother's soiled sheets, towels her body off in her sleep, the toxic sweat oozing from her dilated pores clinging to his skin when he repositions her in bed. He tells Barbara and me we have to stop feeding her. She is passing on, and it will be less painful for her. Barbara hugs him and cries, and I see how difficult it is for them to starve a woman they seem to love so much, to watch her skin sliding out of place as she disappears behind it, pound by pound. I want to get there, to feel that sadness like any halfway decent person would when their mother is dying right before their eyes. But something inside me is blocked up. I realize all the time I should have been preparing for Mama Su's death I've been running away into Clay's arms, the safety and warmth of his room. I've spent all my time at my mother's watching Clay read her his poetry, holding her head up when she thinks she's about to die, being the child she could've had if she hadn't been so unforgivable for most of her life. And all the while these things are happening to her, I've been watching him. He takes my presence as devotion, but really I want to run, and only stay because of the magnetism I feel between him and me. I realize, if he weren't here, I wouldn't be either. But the time has come when I must be truly present, and I can't. In her last moments, Mama Su's fingers reach for me on the duvet, too weak to lift more than an inch. "I can't," I say. "I just can't."

I run outside and retch in the bushes, crying because everything is so ugly, and I don't want to be here where I will surely be found out. Clay comes outside and holds my trembling body close to his, wiping the tears from my face, cooing, "Hey, hey, hey. . ." thinking I am genuinely grieving for my mother.

"I know how hard this must be for you." Without realizing what I'm doing, I step back and slap Clay as hard as I can across his beautiful face. He doesn't look away. He doesn't even flinch.

"You don't know shit," I say. Then it all comes out, everything I've been holding back, because I want him to know, before she dies, what Mama Su is really like and what I'm going through now because of it. So I tell him about growing up at my grandmother's after Mama Su dumped me there, how I'd written a novel about everything that'd happened, how my mother had read it, "and the most fucked up thing about it was," I tell him, "after she read it, she says, 'That's not how it happened.' Like she would know. Like she was there! She was never there. She knew what it was like there, and she left me there to rot."

Clay is looking at me, not lustfully or courageously, but with genuine empathy. And even though I know I should quit, should let him come to me and hold me, I want to see how honest I can be with him, to push him away to see if he'll come back, if he'll forgive me.

"I'm not going back in there. I'm not sad for her. I'm glad," I shout, wanting Clay to hear every syllable. "I'm glad she's dying. I hate her. And I hate that you think you know her, know me. You're just some dumb kid who doesn't know how lucky he is that everyone he knows is already dead, because when someone's dead, they can't fuck you up." Clay looks hurt and somehow smaller, and I don't know if it's what I've said or Mama Su's sickness that's washed him out, but he's fading before my eyes. I've slashed and burned, and all that's left is exhausted, ashen, Clay. I want to say what he needs to hear to bring him back, but he won't look at me. Not even when he reaches out his hand and touches my shoulder for the last time.

"Keep the shirt," he says. And I realize what he means is, "Go kill yourself, Lola."

Leeches

You spilled your grief into my mouth one night over drinks. Alone in your apartment, you bolted your doors and made me a rose-colored cocktail in a tall, green glass. As you shuffled in the kitchen, the silver static under your feet felt like hummingbirds under my tongue; I didn't know what not to say. I asked about the river that flowed through our two hometowns, one thousand one hundred miles apart. One summer you saw a cow corpse, wrapped in wire, come down from the mountains in an avalanche of melted snow. You saved an orphaned bird in the field where your horse was buried, and when your father drove his car into the side of his barn you no longer lay with God-fearing women. I swam naked through the tepid waters of your memories, keeping my eyes open, always open underwater, never fearing the by then calm waters, and came up with leeches, the teeth of that season sinking into my flesh. Our clothes fell in heaps to the floor like freshly dug graves. In your drowsy yellow room, I felt the slither of leeches under your skin, heard the voices of those who died flushing through your arteries, while your fugitive blood blushed like flowers under my skin. And so it was that I decided to stay over, because everything was perfect, and you had been accumulating in my blood since before I knew you, before I knew what it was to love bathed in the flood of another's terrible summer.

Little Ways

I've dared to keep you, even though it means you witness time ruin me in little ways you'd miss in the veil of a one-night stand: this age spot here, a chipped tooth, mornings I couldn't get out of bed. Some days my eyes trick me. I think I've lost it all. But desire is close. You are close.

Acknowledgements

Gracias a mi padre, and my mother, for sustaining me. For your endless strength, thank you.

To all my dear ones, Dirk, Karlee, Lara, Anthony, Kris, Jennifer, Kacy, India, Danielle, Michael, Kate, Chris, Tammy, Bradley, Rebecca, Bradford, Sofía, Austin, Fisayo, Margaret, Evan, Cheeto and Travis, thank you. You've encouraged me, shown me the greatest generosity, and have enriched my life beyond measure. You are my family and my community. I love you.

Then there are those whom I must thank every chance I get for the rest of my life for helping shape this collection in the best and biggest ways: Iris Smyles, Carolina de Robertis, Peter Orner, Michael Krasny, Junse Kim, Andrew Joron, Chanan Tigay, Peter Schmidt, and Jill Gladstein. Thank you for giving my writing a chance, and for inspiring me every day with your dedication to the art of writing!

Thank you Fourteen Hills Press! Thank you Red Light Lit, Litquake, Beast Crawl, Voz Sin Tinta, Bay Area Generations, Pan Dulce Poets, and VelRo, for giving these stories a home before they had ink.

Thank you Kate McNamara for creating wondrous woodcut printings for several of these stories.

Danielle Truppi and Bradley Penner, thank you for designing this beautiful book, and for bringing my dream into the light.

I am so grateful to the spirit and memory of Michael Rubin, and for all the books that exist because of him. It's an honor to carry this torch.

Thank you Texas and California and Mexico and España and Swarthmore and every beautiful place on this fantastic planet. May no border ever keep us from each other.

And you.

All of my love, all of you have it.

Loria Mendoza hails from Austin, Texas, where she learned to keep it weird. Seeking the constancy of the bizarre, she moved to the Mission District in San Francisco, where she earned her MFA in the Creative Writing program at San Francisco State University. Her work has been published or is forthcoming in *Mobius, Subprimal, Maudlin House, Red Light Lit, The Walrus Literary Journal, Transfer Magazine,* and featured at Voz Sin Tinta, Bay Area Generations, Pan Dulce Poets, MFA Mixer 2.0, Velro, Oakland's Beast Crawl and San Francisco's Litquake. She lives in Austin, again.